HITTING THE HIGHEST NOTES

A SYMPHONY OF IDEAS TO HELP
YOU REACH YOUR FULL
POTENTIAL

BEVERLY SALLEE

PREMIERE
TRAINING
CONCEPTS

12/05

Book Packaging and Design: W. B. Freeman Concepts, Tulsa, Oklahoma

Printed in the United States of America
13 12 11 10 09 08 07 06 05 2 3 4 5

ISBN (paper): 0-9760881-0-X

DEDICATION

To
my daughter Debi
my son-in-law Mark
my son Paul

PREFACE

In recent years especially, women seem to have gained a great deal of self-fulfillment as professional business opportunities have opened up to them around the world. More than ever, we women face the challenge of sorting out our success so as to make the most of each day's adventures and celebrations.

From my perspective, this book is a "symphony of ideas and solutions" to help you become a powerhouse of love, faith, respect, caring, and satisfaction. I trust this book will help you move into new vistas of opportunity.

One of my passions is to learn about highly dedicated and productive women through the generations who have changed our world. Some of their stories are told in this book. The list of women whose lives are marked by high achievement is a long one. But the list is not yet complete. There's still room for you and for me to be on it! NOTE TO MEN: There's something for you to learn here, too! The more you understand, encourage and help the women with whom you work, the greater you and your business will become.

Your life and achievements *should* be something your family members and friends celebrate for decades to come. What a legacy you can leave as a woman who reached her full potential!

My hope for you is that regardless of the endeavors you are involved in, or what age you may be, your life will be one of significance and meaning.

— BEVERLY SALLEE

CONTENTS

Letting
Your Spirit Soar

Success based on anything but internal
fulfillment is bound to be empty.

—Dr. Martha Friedman

I love it when something happens that makes my spirit soar.

You know the feeling.

Suddenly you are experiencing an awesome wonder...the manifestation of a stellar talent...the expression of a pure heart...the majesty of creation's splendor...the thrill of being in the presence of near-perfection.

For me, spirit-soaring moments occur most predictably when I am listening to a musical performance and the performer is "on song," as the English say so beautifully. That is especially true when the performer is a classical soprano and she hits the high notes with a clarity and purity of tone that sends chills running down the spine and causes an audience to leap to its collective feet with spontaneous applause and cheers!

This is a book primarily for and about women, so the metaphor of a soprano is appropriate. And because I am a musician at heart and by training, the metaphor of music will run throughout this book. There's a soul song for you to sing—a song titled "your success" that has a melody of joy and a rhythm of satisfaction. It's a song only you can sing. It's a success only you can achieve. And when you do...your spirit will soar and others will be inspired to follow your example.

Your Song of Success

Every woman has an inborn drive for success. She may not be able to articulate it or write it down, but every woman is always trying to succeed at something. That something, whatever it may be, propels a woman's thoughts, feelings, and actions. Every woman is constantly focused on what she wants to accomplish, even if she doesn't consciously realize it.

Our concept of success is developed and conditioned over many years. We come to this concept by what our family members tell us they value, what our peers and associates are striving to achieve, what the media holds out as a picture of "successful," and what we

ourselves have experienced. The net effect is a mix of positive and negative. We drive ourselves *positively* toward those things that we hope will build our self-esteem and our ability to both feel and express love, happiness, and peace of mind. We push ourselves away from the negatives—those experiences and temptations that we either know or suspect could lead to our downfall or a setback.

Three of the most important questions you can ever ask yourself about your own drive for success are these:

- What song do I really want to sing in my life? In other words, what do I really want to accomplish?

- To whom, with whom, and for whom do I desire to sing my success song? A song *is* still a song, even if there's no audience…but that just isn't the way life works. We all are in relationship with others and there's *always* an audience listening to you, watching you, and learning from you. In most cases, there are others who sing harmony with you—family members, close friends, or co-workers who sing along.

- How can I train and prepare myself to hit the highest notes—in other words, to be my best, do my best, and achieve the most?

People seek answers to these questions throughout their lives. No one ever fully answers every question and there are no definitive one-size-fits-all answers. You must pursue the answers that are right for you, but let me quickly reassure you that answers can be found. You *can* sing a success song that is uniquely your own.

Success Myths

Two of the great myths about success are myths commonly applied to music. Let me address them at the outset of this book:

- **Musicians Are Born, Not Made.** No one is born a professional musician. And no woman is born with the silver

spoon of success in her mouth! Every professional performer has had to learn music and hone the craft of musicianship. The same is true for those who are successful. Certain principles must be learned, applied, and practiced. You may not be as successful today as you'd like to be...but you can learn to become *more* successful. You may not even believe you have very much potential...but you can learn how to discover your potential and develop it.

A student once said to me, "I just don't have any musical ability." The person who said this was an adult. My first inclination was to respond, "You didn't think that when you were in kindergarten." Every child I've ever met has known how to sing, dance, and at a very early age, beat out a rhythm with a spoon on a high chair's tray! Every person has the potential for GREAT success. Don't lose sight of who you have been created to become.

- **Music Is All About Emotion.** Music is actually very rational and mathematical. There are only so many beats to a measure and notes in the scale. Different styles of music and types of composition follow highly prescribed rules. Success, likewise, is not an emotion-driven process. There are certain elements that will make a person successful in any given field—a salesperson, for example, needs to make calls; an author needs to meet deadlines with a prescribed number of pages or words; an airline pilot needs to run through a checklist before takeoff; and so forth. Success doesn't happen either by whim or hype—it happens by *will*.

The Song that YOU Sing

No one has your voice but *you*.

You are a "whole" person. You have emotional, physical, spiritual, mental, and relational sides to your being. You have both feelings and the ability to reason. You have dreams, aspirations, and desires

related to various realms of your life—business, family, and community. All of these aspects of you as an individual, as well as all the aspects of how you relate to the world around you, are intertwined.

I don't believe it is accurate to call yourself successful if one area of your life is crying out, "No success here!" A successful life is one marked by balance and harmony, which is only possible if a woman has a life that is rooted in real and lasting values.

Furthermore, I personally do not know a woman who WANTS to succeed in business and fail in marriage. I also don't know a woman who wants to succeed in marriage and yet fail miserably in the practical areas of life. Those who achieve great levels of excellence in business have very few FEELINGS of success if they are burned out physically and emotionally. For success to be genuine, you must be successful in ALL areas of your life.

"But you can't have it all," you may be saying.

Oh yes, you can! I believe very strongly you were meant to have it all. The key is having it all *correctly,* which means in balance and harmony, with meaning and purpose, and with deep inner joy and feelings of fulfillment.

This book is based upon three very simple assumptions I make about you and every woman I've ever met:

1. Every woman wants a life with solid values and meaningful relationships.

2. Every woman wants a life that is based upon a satisfying sense of purpose—she wants to sing a song *worth* singing.

3. Every woman wants a life of joy, based upon doing pleasurable work and receiving pleasurable rewards.

How do we get that life we want? That's what this book is about! Just as there are "laws" related to good music composition, so there are some essentials required in order for you to sing your finest

song. Using the letters associated with the musical scale, these essentials are:

A = Action. If you are to reach your full potential in life, you must DO something. You must grab hold of life and be proactive. The person who sits idly by and watches the years and opportunities pass is not a woman who will fulfill her destiny.

B = Balance. A cart that's missing one wheel isn't going anywhere—at least not anywhere fast. For you to get the most out of life and produce the most in your life, you need to live a balanced life.

C = Character. There is no genuine success unless you have a reputation as a person with values and integrity.

D = Destiny. Every woman has a destiny to fulfill—a plan and purpose for her life that needs to be discovered and pursued. Destiny is "potential…defined."

E = Energy. Every person has a spiritual core. How you develop your spiritual and emotional energy will determine how far you go, and how high you soar.

F = Focus. There is no great orchestra performance unless every musician is on the "same page." Music has a cadence to it—a rhythm, a sequence, an unfolding of melody. The same is true of life. To get to a goal, you must stay focused and remain disciplined.

G = Giving and Growing. I chose two words for this final principle because they are interrelated. Those who give, grow. Those who are growing in a balanced, comprehensive way are ultimately those who become givers.

These principles work synergistically—in other words, they work together to create a whole that is more powerful than a mere "summing up" of the parts. A single note sung repeatedly does not make a song—a chant perhaps, but not a lyrical song. Notes work together in rhythm, harmony, and sequence to create music, and in the same way, the principles identified above work together in a powerful way to produce fruit in your life: balance, fulfillment, and joy.

Practice Perfects

We've all heard the phrase, "Practice makes perfect." Rarely is any performance perfect. A more accurate phrase would be, "Practice *perfects*." Practice helps you become *better* at anything you attempt to do, including thinking the right thoughts and developing the right beliefs and values.

In any discipline, principles need to be applied. At the close of each chapter, therefore, I invite you to a "practice session"—an opportunity to act on some of the principles presented to you. Let's get started! Here's your first Practice Session....

———————— Practice Session ————————

1. Write out your own obituary. Spend a few minutes thinking about how it is that YOU want to be remembered. Put your thoughts into writing! Then ask, "Does this match up with the way I am currently living?"

2. Write out, in a statement of fifty words or less, your answer to this question: "At the end of my life, how will I know if I have SUCCEEDED at reaching my potential?"

3. Evaluate yourself on the seven principles below:

 = open, free, blooming

= budding and becoming

= tired, wilted, not succeeding

A = ACTION . . . .

I am a woman of action! I don't sit and wait for things to happen—I make them happen.

B = BALANCE . . . .

I live a life that is in good balance—family, friends, work, physical health, spiritual life, emotional life, finances, and learning.

C = CHARACTER . . . .

I have a strong belief system that produces integrity and character.

D = DESTINY . . . .

I am steadily pursuing a "mission" or a "potential... defined" for my life.

E = ENERGY . . . .

I continually "recharge" my own spiritual core.

F = FOCUS . . . . I routinely review my priorities. I am committed to staying focused as I pursue my goals and develop my potential.

G = GIVING and GROWING . . . . I am always looking for and seizing opportunities to give to others and to grow in all areas of my life.

Spend some time reflecting on those areas in which you are "wilting."

Action

Seizing the Moment and Sustaining the Effort

*Life is about not knowing,
having to change, taking the moment and
making the best of it, without
knowing what's going to happen next.*

—GILDA RADNER, COMEDIENNE

CHAPTER

2

Renee had the world in the palm of her hand. She was young and vibrant and each day she shared her passion for music with young people as a choir director in a Southern California high school. She was also planning her wedding. She didn't know what challenges a new day might bring, but good things were happening in her life. Her future was filled with promise and she was filled with hope.

Her life changed overnight…literally. Two months before her wedding, Renee fell out of bed in a freak accident and instantly became a quadriplegic. When her fiancé heard the news, he prayed, "Lord, don't let her die. I don't care if there is a chair, just don't let her die."

When he walked into her hospital room, he smiled and said, "Hi, honey, we can do this." Renee smiled back and said, "I guess we'll always have a good parking space." A year later they were married.

Attitude made all the difference in Renee's life. Good things had been happening to her prior to her accident, but when the road became rocky, she didn't lose heart or faith. Instead, she believed that good things could continue to happen. She went after her hopes and dreams with a vengeance.

With the help of a vocal coach friend, Renee began to lift weights on her diaphragm. After five months in the hospital she was able to lift fifty-five pounds, which enabled her to sing again. She soon was sharing her passion for music with young people as the director of the children's choir at the mission in San Juan Capistrano. She recorded several albums and began traveling to give concerts. In 1995 she was able to give birth to a child; at the time she was the "highest quadriplegic level" in the United States ever to do this.

Today, Renee continues to sing and raise her family. Each day she wheels her son, Daniel, into class on the back of her wheelchair. Life is different than Renee ever expected it to be, but it's just as GOOD as she expected. She continues to wake up each morning with an expectancy about what good thing might happen next!

I first met Renee more than twenty years ago when we were both choral conductors. We sang together in the Oregon Bach Festival each summer. Since her accident, I have invited Renee to sing and speak at various business functions, especially those that are attended by teenagers. She continues to inspire me and to do away with any excuse for not overcoming obstacles! The main focus of her message always seems to be this:

You cannot sit around and wait for life to find you.
You have to go get it.
Take responsibility for your thoughts and actions
and go get the future you want for yourself!

Renee is the embodiment of the word "proactive." She is pursuing ALL that life has for her. In her spirit, she is running toward her potential.[1]

Choose to Move Forward

Renee faced a crisis moment that required her to make a choice: sit back, or move forward. She chose to move forward.

What about you?

You may not have a moment when you awaken to find yourself a quadriplegic—I trust you never will have such a moment! But this very moment as you are reading this book may very well be the decisive moment in your life when you *choose* to move forward rather than sit where you are.

A decision to move forward is a conscious, intentional, willful decision. It is not a decision that "just happens."

There are several prerequisites to taking action. Let me share my top six of them with you.

Prerequisite for Action #1:
Let go of anything in your past that is associated with failure.

Accept responsibility for your own actions and attitudes. Lay down the failure of the past and then…move forward!

I certainly am not advocating that you move, divorce, quit your job, or abandon your family. Sometimes people think that to let go of the past, they need to pack the car and leave town. That isn't at all what's necessary, at least in the vast majority of cases.

What you *do* need to do is let go of the past in your mind.

You won't be effective in driving into your future if you continue to stare into the rearview mirror.

If you are shackled by thoughts of someone who has taken something from you or rejected you…forgive that person and move forward.

If you are bound up by the bad opinions of a person who criticized you or continually put you down…speak to that person even if the person isn't in the room: "What you said to me was a lie. I refuse to believe that lie any longer. I'm moving forward into the truth."

If you are tied down by memories of abuse…take a long look at yourself in the mirror and tell yourself, "I am a valuable person. What was done to me was evil. I didn't deserve it. There's something better ahead for me." Every time a memory of that abuse comes back to haunt you, take charge of your own thinking and *choose* to think about something positive you expect to receive or enjoy in the future.

Let go of anything that you can't control.

Don't let worries, anxieties, or situations that are beyond your control keep you in a straightjacket. Focus only on those things that *you* can determine—your attitudes, your feelings, your beliefs, your words, and your behaviors.

One of the finest examples of this I know is the life of Sarah Breedlove.

Sarah was born free, but just barely. She was born on a cotton plantation in Delta, Louisiana, about five years after the Emancipation Proclamation was issued. She and her slave-born brothers and sister had little, if any, hope for formal education or a prosperous future.

By age seven Sarah was an orphan living with her older sister and abusive brother-in-law. As a ten-year-old, Sarah began working in the homes of white families as a laundress. To escape this life she married Moses McWilliams at age fourteen and had a daughter at age seventeen. Three years later, Moses died.

Determined to make a better life for herself and her daughter, Sarah "Sallie" McWilliams paid four dollars for passage on a steamboat headed to St. Louis. Relegated to the cramped cargo area, surrounded by livestock and the deafening noise of the vibrating engine, Sarah went in search of a future.

Once in St. Louis, Sarah spent the next decade working as a washerwoman, always dreaming of a better life but not knowing quite how to achieve it. She moved, sometimes as many as three times a year, from one damp, cold room to another in the dangerous neighborhood in which she lived. She bounced from one abusive relationship to another, seemingly unable to extricate herself from a life of poverty and failure.

Sarah attended the St. Paul AME church, and there, she began to observe closely the mannerisms, conversations, and outward signs of wealth in the middle-class black congregants. She was motivated by what she observed, and a desire for success began to grow in her heart. It was at St. Paul's that she also began to develop social skills while doing good deeds with the missionary society. She took advantage of the opportunities that presented themselves and created leadership roles for herself within the church by raising money for families in need.

As Sarah continued to improve herself on the inside with a more self-assured attitude and inner confidence, she began to desire improvement on the outside. Sarah had started to lose her hair while she was still a young woman. At the turn of the twentieth century this was a common complaint for many women. Illness, scalp disease, low-protein diets, and damaging hair treatments were mostly to blame. Stress caused by abuse was also a likely factor in Sarah's case. Sarah wore her hair closely cropped to her head with a small puff of bangs above her forehead to hide her hair loss. That style, however, was not the fashion of the day.

The Gibson Girl look was all the rage—long, silky tresses, dainty Cupid's bow lips, and a tiny waist. Women of all races and stations in life tried to reach this ideal, as unattainable as it may have been for most.

Sarah took a few lessons in hygiene and began performing some late-night experiments with natural and exotic ingredients. She soon perfected a mixture that grew hair! She shared her formula with her daughter and neighbors, and very quickly, Sarah realized that her hair-growing preparation was destined to be her ticket out of poverty. As her hair grew long and luxurious, she began to make plans to sell her formula.

Sarah McWilliams was now Sallie Walker as the result of a marriage to a man named C. J. Walker. She adopted her new husband's initials and tacked Madam onto the front of her name. Madam C. J. Walker's Wonderful Hair Grower was launched and soon was being distributed nationwide.

Madam Walker's success was not just in the formula she created and manufactured. She had a strong belief that all women want to be attractive and have a measure of self-worth. She had an equally strong belief that women need to be financially independent.

Madam Walker established agents across the nation who could sell her products and compete for prizes and awards, thus supporting themselves and their families. Awards were given not only for sales prowess but also for philanthropic works. Madam C. J. Walker envisioned a national sales force "expressly organized around the principles of corporate responsibility, social betterment, and racial justice." She was a dynamic force for these principles during the first two decades of the twentieth century. And, she created an empire of titanic proportions.

By the time Madam Walker died in 1920, she had traveled across the United States and in the Caribbean, teaching her hair-growing techniques to women of all backgrounds and colors. She had rubbed elbows with America's elite, both black and white, and had become a world-renowned philanthropist. In today's economy her fortune would have been worth $6 million. She left a legacy of educating women about beauty, business, politics, and foreign affairs.[2]

If a child born on a plantation just a few years away from slavery could overcome what Madam Walker overcame...if an abused, poorly educated woman with a string of failures could rise to the top...there are no excuses! Let go of anything that smacks of failure in your past and face today as a NEW day of opportunity.

Prerequisite for Action #2:
Adopt an "I can"... "I must" ... "I WILL" attitude.

There's a great Dennis the Menace cartoon in which Dennis is sitting in a chair facing the corner of a room as a punishment. He looks over his shoulder at his mother and says, "I may be sitting down on the outside, but I am standing up on the inside."

See yourself in that way. Realistically, you may be broke...hurt... wounded...discouraged...or poor. Refuse, however, to see this as a permanent state of being. INSIDE, see yourself as healed, strong, vibrant, on top of life, and prospering. Stand up on the inside! Get moving, motivate others around you to move, and soon you *will* be on your way to the life you want.

Early in my career I taught choral music at an inner-city high school in the greater Los Angeles area. Many of the students were highly talented. They seemed to be trapped, however, in a cycle of poverty and defeat. The majority of them didn't know their fathers. Some came from homes where there wasn't enough food or where they were being raised by mothers or grandmothers who had no time to listen to them.

I quickly discovered that many of my conversations with these young people had little to do with music and everything to do with making choices. I found that my greatest challenge was helping them see that they had talents and abilities, and then helping them discover how they might develop those talents and abilities to achieve success. I focused on teaching them to change what they could change, and let go emotionally and mentally of what they couldn't change.

This same message is one that works in the business world. Stand up and change what you can change. Let go of the rest!

Elisa Pritzker is a woman who did just that. She was an international artist and curator in Argentina. She also spent time in Spain. Then she moved to Highland, New York, a community of about ten thousand people that had no art galleries or art programs. She felt herself "drying up" as an artist.

Elisa could have sat down and said, "Woe is me. How did I end up in this sleepy town with no cultural life?" She could have tried to escape. She could have blamed her limited fluency in English or a lack of access to big-city cultural activities for her personal misery. Instead, she stood up on the inside and took action. She and her husband began to organize art activities for children. Within a year, she obtained nonprofit status for the Highland Community Center arts project. She began to offer classes and workshops in a downtown gallery, and in the summer, HCC-Arts began a summer music festival. Today, local performers and artists share their talents with more than twenty thousand people in the mid-Hudson Valley region. The Center has become a focal point for the community.[3]

What might you do if you simply took the step of standing up on the inside with a goal of changing something you do not like—either something you don't like in yourself or something you don't like in the world around you?

What you choose to do may very well become the legacy you leave for generations to come. It won't happen, however, if you continue to sit and stare into the corner of your life.

Prerequisite for Action #3:
Accept responsibility for motivating YOURSELF.

Many people I've met through the years expect other people to motivate them to greatness. They attend conferences with arms crossed, almost daring a speaker to "charge them up." They wait for their spouse to come up with the "next idea"—which might be the "next date," the "next party," the "next goal." The truth is, ultimately, only *you* can motivate you.

Certainly you can avail yourself of all the opportunities to hear motivational speakers, but you are the one who has to listen, take notes, and receive into your heart and mind what that speaker has to say to you. You can buy motivational and inspirational tapes, but you are the one who has to pop those tapes and CDs into their players, listen to them, and process them in your brain.

No one is going to do the work of motivation in your life but you. You and you alone know what motivates you, what sets your heart to humming and your mind to spinning, what "lights your fire." You are the one who has those deep, hidden dreams and desires for your own life lying dormant in your soul, and ultimately, you are the one who has to awaken those dreams and desires and search for a way to turn them into a reality.

I learned this lesson after a lot of years and a few tears.

Growing up, I was the child who organized neighborhood projects, motivated the troops, and got all the other kids moving. If there was a wide variety of activities to participate in, I opted to participate in *all* of them!

In the fourth grade I organized the neighborhood children to dig a big hole in my backyard so we could have a swimming pool. This lasted several days…until they got tired of my supervising and their digging, and my father put a stop to the whole project. Another time I convinced all the kids on my block to build a tree house in a tall willow tree behind our neighbor's house. I instructed all the kids to swing down from the tree Tarzan-style. Of course, I didn't tell anyone I was too afraid to climb up the tree and swing down myself. In that situation, I was better at telling than doing.

This ability to get people moving appealed to me later in life. I studied to become a teacher because I saw teaching as an opportunity to organize, challenge, and make something happen.

This desire to get things done and see things happen later became a major factor in my business success.

But first, before I could motivate anyone else to move forward, I had to move forward MYSELF.

As a music teacher, my greatest motivational tool in teaching others to play the piano and to sing was the fact that *I* had learned to play the piano and sing! I didn't just tell others to sing…I sang along. I didn't just tell others the notes to play…I showed them.

One day I sat down with a reluctant piano student and said, "You want to play like this, don't you?" and I launched into a fast, showy piece with lots of runs up and down the keyboard. The student eagerly said, "Oh yes, that's the way I want to play!"

I then began to play a simple five-finger scale over and over. "In order to play like that someday, you have to play like this today," I said. "You can't play like I just played until you first learn to play the scales like I'm playing them now."

Show and tell is still the best way to teach and motivate.

As a person in business, I first had to succeed at selling before I could motivate others to sell.

I've learned through the years that I'm only successful in teaching and selling when *other people*—my students or my business associates—begin to motivate *themselves* to move forward. When I no longer need to do the motivating, and they are motivating themselves, I know they truly are on their way.

The simple fact is this: To make things happen for or with others, you must first make things happen in yourself! Start with you, and then seek to influence others.

Become Motivated by Your Vision of the BEST LIFE. There are few things as motivating as having a vision for what is the BEST.

There are those who claim that "goals" motivate a person. I believe that is true, but only if the goal is rooted in what a person believes is the "highest and best" life has to offer. When you have a vision for what is the BEST option, choice, or course of action in any given situation, you will be motivated to pursue the BEST.

Ask yourself routinely:

"What can I do to make the BEST of this situation or circumstance?"

What is the BEST thing you can say?

What is the BEST thing you can do?

What is the BEST idea you have to offer?

What is the BEST way you can show that you care?

What is the BEST you can give?

What is the BEST service you can provide?

What is the BEST way to go about solving the problem?

What is the BEST possible decision or solution for everyone involved?

Excellence is a habit worthy of practice!

Take a look around you. There are many intelligent, talented, and highly skilled people in this world who aren't succeeding in realizing their potential. Their lives are marked by a lack of balance, a lack of inner peace, a lack of fulfillment and feelings of purpose. They aren't hitting the high notes. Why? In most cases, it's because they have seen excellence as something they pursue only in their work or in developing their personal talent. The greater truth is that if they saw excellence as something related to the totality of their life, and they pursued excellence in all things, they would truly find success.

Are you pursuing excellence in your friendships?

Are you pursuing excellence in your personal habits?

Are you pursuing excellence in your relationship with God?

Are you pursuing the excellence of your mind...your heart... your talents...your career?

Are you taking into your life the most excellent ideas... inspiration...and "input"?

Are you giving out your most excellent effort, your personal BEST?

If you truly are going to pursue your potential, first make sure that what you are seeking to accomplish is the BEST life has to offer! Choose to be motivated by what is superlative.

Prerequisite for Action #4:
Lay down the attitudes that keep you
from taking action.

If you truly are going to realize your potential, you must lay down the "Big Three" attitudes that will keep you from taking action:

• **Bad Attitude #1. Others exist to serve me.** It takes conscious effort to get over an "I'm the center of the universe" attitude. "Me first" comes automatically—just watch any two-year-old in action! Children instinctively cling to objects they consider to be theirs. One of the first words that children learn is "Mine!" It is not automatic for us to have an attitude, "Others first. Others count. Consider others. Serve others."

What is the danger of being self-absorbed? You will WAIT for others to serve you…to do for you what only you can do for yourself…to "make things happen FOR you." And the truth is, they never will. Not fully. Not consistently. Not in a way that is truly satisfying to you throughout your life.

There are those who are quick to exclaim, "Look out for Number One!" What's wrong with doing so? Those who follow this path have little love and joy in their lives. Instead, they have a restlessness that never seems to be satisfied. They rarely have fulfilling relationships or genuine joy.

Certainly, in very small doses, self-gratification and a desire for "more" can be good. When a job has been done well, there is a natural amount of pride that should be felt. A person should be able to say to herself, "Good job!"—even if nobody else says it. In small doses, self-gratification can be a great incentive. We need to give ourselves small rewards to stay motivated. The setting of goals to accomplish more in life can also be motivating.

What we must ask ourselves is, "Am I hindering or furthering my progress in reaching my ultimate goals by indulging in this reward or feeling this feeling?"

A person who has a goal of helping others make their sales quota is going to be greatly *hindered* by a self-absorbed attitude, especially if those people she should be helping are in her own organization!

A person who has a goal of being healthy and looking her best is going to be *hindered* by giving herself a self-gratifying reward of overeating.

A person who has a goal of living debt-free is going to be *hindered* by maxing out her credit cards during a shopping spree at the mall.

It takes discipline to rein in one's thoughts and be humble, generous, and patient when it comes to rewards and gratification. The more a person practices these attitudes, however, the easier it becomes to maintain these thought processes. Eventually, they become "automatic" and take less effort.

- **Bad Attitude #2. I have plenty of time.** Maybe so, but…maybe not.

  Your future isn't as far away as you may think. It isn't off on the distant horizon. It's TODAY. How you successfully live today determines your success tomorrow. The future you desire is in your hands right now. Focus your strength and perseverance on living TODAY in the way you want to live the rest of your life.

  Live out the hours of TODAY according to your principles and core beliefs. Live out TODAY with the priorities you want to have forever. Live out TODAY with your goals clearly in mind and your determination set to trade in weaknesses for strengths.

  You have what it takes to live a genuinely successful life TODAY. And once today has been lived according to your vision of the BEST LIFE…live tomorrow in the same fashion. The future will unfold in just the way you want it to unfold.

- **Bad Attitude #3. I must not be cut out for success.** Most people simply give up too quickly. Very often, they give up just when they are on the brink of success. Why do you assume that your business can't be turned around? Why do you assume that you will never lose the weight you want to lose? Why do you assume that your marriage is doomed to failure, or that you will never find the right spouse?

There are a number of reasons that people feel they are destined for failure. Very often these feelings are linked to past rejection, past criticism (feelings of unworthiness), and past poor performance. The successful person, however, is the person who says, "I AM cut out for success and therefore, I'm going to pursue it with all I have."

Angelica Guevara is just such a person. She grew up in a tough neighborhood in Los Angeles. Her parents were both alcoholics who spoke no English and relied on a monthly welfare check to make ends meet. Sometimes things were so tight, there wasn't enough money for rent and food, so Angelica often did her homework late into the night on an empty stomach.

Living in a gang-infested section of the city was dangerous. Angelica survived with the help of her older brother, who put the word out on the street that she was not to be bothered or harassed. In high school she became known on the streets as "the school girl" because, while working nights and weekends to help support her family, she also carried a full load of college preparatory courses including Advanced Placement statistics, physics, and honors chemistry.

In elementary school Angelica did not stand out as a gifted student. She made mostly C's and D's. But when she was in fifth grade, a teacher saw her standardized test scores and noticed how articulate she was in both English and Spanish. The teacher encouraged Angelica to enroll in a magnet school for gifted students. Angelica felt out of place among the mostly white and Asian students in her new school, but she stayed. She began to get a vision for her potential and she embraced the possibility that a life outside the "projects" was attainable through education.

During high school things were tougher than ever at home. Angelica was pressured by her mother to quit school and get a job. Money was so tight that during her three years in high school, she only had one pair of shoes. Her brother helped her keep the soles nailed together so they wouldn't fall off. Once, when the family's welfare check didn't come, Angelica asked fellow students for donations of food and money just so she could eat. "It's the hardest thing I've ever had to do," she said. "I hated asking for help, but I saw no other way out." Her classmates helped with food and a hundred dollars.

Angelica graduated from high school with a 3.9 grade-point average, seven college scholarships, and a late-summer start date at UCLA. Angelica hasn't "arrived" yet, but she's already a successful person because she chooses to believe that NOTHING can or will stand in her way.[4]

- **The Flip Side.** Here is the flip side of the three attitudes I've described above:
  - "There's somebody who needs what only I can give."
  - "I can't wait."
  - "I have a destiny that must be realized."

Adopt these three attitudes and you'll be READY for action!

Prerequisite for Action #5:
Be willing to work.

Changing attitudes and pursuing positive goals requires WORK. Making things happen takes WORK. There is no substitute for good, honest, hard work.

A man named Robert Thornton Henderson once said, "Most of the significant things done in the world were done by persons who were either too busy or too sick. There are few ideal and leisurely settings for the disciplines of growth." I couldn't agree more. A "setting" or "environment" is NOT what leads to change. Hard work and effort are required, and especially so in adverse conditions.

I grew up with a sound work ethic. Our family worked together to achieve our goals. At one point my father bought a dairy. My sister and I were expected to help with the chores before and after school. Later, my father built houses…so we did, too. Today, I am grateful for those experiences because they taught me important lessons about work. Our hard work made a difference in our lives, as well as in the lives of people around us. Even as children we "made things happen."

One of the hottest sports tickets today is the WUSA, the Women's United Soccer Association. The popularity of women's soccer has skyrocketed in the last few years. The players who are in this league, however, did not just suddenly appear overnight on the international stage. They worked for years and years, perfecting their skills through daily practice and countless games. They traveled in old buses and stayed in cheap motels as they played game after game in city after city. Today, thousands of spectators and little girls everywhere know the names of the greats: Mia Hamm, Brandy Chastain, Michelle Akers, and others. These are women who worked HARD even when they didn't get the recognition warranted by their talents. They pushed through the rough times and changed women's sports forever.

There are four aspects of work I want to underscore for you:

1. **Continue to work even when the road gets rough.** When you work through the hard times, you emerge stronger and more resilient. If you give up in hard times, the work you have done fails to produce and you are likely to develop a "failure mindset" rather than a strong "success mindset." You MUST work through times of setback, rejection, lack of recognition, and difficulties if you are going to succeed.

2. **Become passionate about your work.** Countless women go to work every day simply to "make money," and because they have no real passion for the work they are doing and the goals they are attempting to accomplish, they work in a halfhearted and dispirited way. Their work lacks excellence, energy, and creativity. In the end, they feel miserable and unfulfilled. Choose to work at something you can become passionate about.

3. **Find work that fits who you are.** Find work that fits your God-given talents and desires. If you are good with children and you draw meaning and purpose from working with young children, then get a job that allows you to work with young children—don't sit behind a desk pushing paper. If you have a creative talent and draw deep inner satisfaction from working in a creative job, find a job in which you can be creative—don't work on an assembly line.

4. **Find work that is FUN.** I have met a number of women who work at rather mundane jobs. Once they are "off the clock," they spend time calling their friends and meeting them for coffee, working in their gardens, or doing projects that they believe will beautify their homes. Work hours are something they associate with drudgery and have-to-have relationships. Off-work hours are something they associate with fun and want-to-have relationships. How much better it is to pursue work that is fun for you and that is infused with good relationships!

Prerequisite for Action #6: Sustain the process—STAY in gear!

All of the steps I've covered up to this point are not onetime activities or experiences. They are part of an ongoing, total process.

You can't just let go of the past once. Tomorrow you will need to let go of *today's* mistakes! To take charge of your life and reach your full potential you need to let go of your mistakes quickly. Learn from them all you can learn, vow not to repeat them, and then move on! Don't let a mistake tie you up in knots.

It's not enough to have an "I can do it" or "I must do it" attitude on one occasion, or concerning one task. You need to get into the habit of approaching all of life's challenges with this attitude. The truth is, if you begin to develop this habit of believing, "I can do this!" you will take on more challenges and risks, avail yourself of more opportunities, and succeed in far greater ways than if you have a habit of saying about each new endeavor, "I can't."

It's not enough to take control of yourself on just one occasion. A disciplined and focused life is a life in which you exert control over your own attitudes and actions on a continual basis.

It's not enough to work hard on one day, or on one project, or in just one area of your life. Hard work must become a habit.

It's not enough to serve others in spurts—a little one day, and then a little two weeks later in another setting. Serving others must become a prevailing attitude, an automatic and immediate response.

Another way of saying "sustain the action" is this: Adopt the HABITS of an action-oriented person.

- **The Habits Worth Developing.** Let me share with you three basic truths about developing habits.

  - **First,** everyone can learn new habits. Habits are formed by repetition and every person is capable of repeating statements or behaviors. It's part of what makes us human beings.

  - **Second,** habits are formed more readily when a person is "accountable" to another person for practicing a habit.

    I know a woman who wanted to build daily exercise into her life. She had a deep desire to lose weight, get fit, have more energy, and look better in her clothes—not necessarily in that order. She realized she didn't know how to use the weight machines at the gym where she went to work out. She got information. She also realized that she needed to have a workout partner, a friend who would walk with her three times a week. She started scheduling her days around workout times. Within three months, working out was a habit for her. If you ask her the key to it all, she will say this: "My exercise partner. If it hadn't been for her encouragement, her presence, and sometimes her nagging, I never would have built the habit of regular exercise into my life."

- **Third,** to build a new habit you need to be able to "see the goal" clearly. My friend who developed the working-out habit hung a swimsuit at the front of her closet. She had a clear goal concerning what she wanted to fit into by summer! If you want higher morale in your department, or a more productive sales force, you must be able to close your eyes and "see" that environment and the ways in which people are relating to one another. If you want your family to have a habit of eating dinner together every night, you need to be able to "see" that picture in your mind.

Ultimately, a habit is fully formed when a person engages in the habit without thinking about it. The habit of working out first thing in the morning is there when the alarm goes off and you instinctively reach for your walking shoes and lace them on. The habit of "reading more and watching less TV" is there when you settle down in your easy chair after dinner and automatically reach for a book instead of the remote control.

The same is true for attitude habits.

You have the attitude of "I can make this happen" when you face a challenge and begin to respond to it *without* first thinking or saying, "I can make this happen!"

You have the attitude of true success when you take charge of a situation *without* first stopping to tell yourself, "I can take charge. I am a responsible person."

You have the attitude of service when you intuitively respond to a person in need *without* first thinking, "Is this a need? Is there anything I should do about it?"

On the front end of developing a new attitude habit, you may need to do a lot of talking to yourself and "pausing to think" about what your response should be. Over time, however, the new attitude habit will become automatic.

- **Keep At It.** Success takes practice. It is like anything in life: We must continually hone our skills for success. We must continue to discipline ourselves to think positively, to work diligently, and to set a forward direction for our lives. We must concentrate on the *process* of achieving our goals, not just on the goals themselves.

  As a musician, I know that a person is in trouble if she quits practicing. The same is true in any other discipline. There are certain things that a person *must continue to do* on a regular, consistent basis if she is going to achieve and then maintain her progress toward any goal she sets.

  Successful writers say they must write…every day.

  Successful artists feel compelled to paint, or sculpt, or design…every day.

  Those who sell must make appointments and make sales presentations and SELL…every day.

  Whatever it is that you define as your area for success, continue to work at it. Continue to build the attitude habits that contribute to your own motivation. Continue to build the daily habits that become lifelong habits. Never stop!

"Forward, March!"

I once visited the Air Force Academy in Colorado Springs, Colorado. I saw the cadets there marching—it seemed to me the entire population of the academy was marching! Cadets marched to class, to recreational activities, to the mess hall…and they especially marched when they got into trouble. The mission of the Air Force cadet is to become a world-class soldier who is able to defend his or her nation with stamina and intelligence. Many go on after graduation to be pilots, members of the Special Forces, and intelligence operatives. The marching they do as young military students not only prepares them for their duties as officers, but it gives them a sense of moving toward their end goal even as they study. Constant forward movement is considered important in keeping them motivated and in helping them keep their ultimate mission in sight.

Approach the accomplishment of your mission in a similar way. Make a commitment to yourself that YOU WILL NOT TURN BACK. Live your life with an attitude of "Forward, march!"

Practice Session

1. Make a choice! On each line below, circle the way you will choose to see yourself as you complete the sentence, "I see myself as…"

Choice A	Choice B
A victim	A victor
Concerned primarily with caring for people	Concerned primarily with completing tasks
Stuck and helpless	Capable and growing
My attitudes are in control of me	I am in control of my attitudes
Disciplined	Undisciplined
Building right attitude habits	Not building right attitude habits
Focused on getting	Focused on giving
Working hard	A little lazy
Settling for mediocrity in some things	Pursuing excellence in all things

Now write out a statement about the person you WANT to be:

I, _____ (your name), choose to be a person
who has these qualities:

2. What is the one attitude that you would most like to change in
   yourself?

How might you go about making that change?

3. Identify one area of your life or your thinking in which you know you need to develop some new habits:

What do you need to do to build up greater DESIRE to acquire this habit?

What INFORMATION do you need?

What SKILLS do you need to develop and practice?

Whom do you need to seek out as an ACCOUNTABILITY partner?

4. Identify one area of your life in which you currently feel as if you are making no forward progress. Describe the way you WANT things to be (in 30 words or less):

What do you need to do to MAKE THAT CHANGE HAPPEN?

5. Read *The Last Dance but Not the Last Song* by Renee Bondi and Nancy Curtis (Fleming H. Revell Company, publisher).

Balance

Successfully Juggling
All Life's Demands

If I had my life to live over again, I would dare to make more mistakes next time. I would relax. I would be sillier. I would take fewer things seriously…I would eat more ice cream and less beans. I would perhaps have more actual troubles but fewer imaginary ones. You see, I'm one of those people who lived seriously and sanely hour after hour, day after day. I've been one of those persons who never went anyplace without a thermometer, a hot water bottle, a raincoat, and a parachute. If I had to do it over again, I'd travel lighter.

—AN 85-YEAR-OLD WOMAN
FROM THE HILL COUNTRY OF KENTUCKY[1]

CHAPTER

3

Elaine Chao is a wife, a leader, a mentor, and the first female Asian-American Cabinet Secretary (nominated by President George H. W. Bush). During her career she has served as the director of the Peace Corps and as president and CEO of the United Way. Secretary Chao has a heart for people, is goal-oriented, and has achieved much success in the world of politics...but she didn't always live a balanced life.

In an article published in *Working Woman*, Secretary Chao was asked how she maintains balance between her personal and professional life. This is what she said:

> It's difficult. I have spent a great deal of my adult life in a career almost to the exclusion of my personal life—not because I purposely didn't want to have a personal life. I was just always so wrapped up in my career...I never made time for it. Then I learned that if my private life was important to me, I had to make it a priority. This meant I had to think about it consciously, make plans for dinner with friends, and affirmatively take action and do something about it.[2]

Life is not one-dimensional. It isn't all about career...or family...or activities. Every woman I know is all too aware of this. The trouble is not getting out of a rut in our life, but rather, juggling all the things we consider important. We want to do everything and be everything, and above all, do it up right!

How can we do it all and find meaning in it all? The key phrase is "harmonious balance." A successful life is a life in which all of the pieces work together to create a balanced and harmonious whole.

Mary Good was dying of colon cancer when she began to see a therapist named Lauren Slater. Mary and Lauren met together because Mary wanted to "reflect back on her life, tie up loose ends, and to use up her insurance benefits before she 'kicked off'!" Lauren found that in spite of the terrible childhood abuse Mary had experienced, she was a woman full of laughter and real joy.

In one of their last meetings, Lauren asked Mary why she wasn't afraid to die. Mary responded, "Death is something to be done with style, and fear is not fashionable." Lauren thought she was equating death with a shopping mall until Mary continued, "You should leave with some sparkle, don't you think? Besides, the thing is, Lauren, I have raised two excellent sons. I have grandsons and a whole family who loves me. When I look back I see I have survived terrible trauma and learned to love despite it. And the funny thing is, the deeper you love, the easier it is to leave."[3]

I agree with Mary. It is not death we fear so much as a poorly lived life. Deep inside all of us, there's a longing for meaning and fulfillment. We want to experience ALL life has to offer: joy, pain, success, failure, fun, stress, and on and on.

Peace and fulfillment come only with *balance* in the totality of life.

Develop Your Understanding of What It Means to Live a Balanced Life

Today many women are excellent multitaskers who juggle a variety of activities on a daily basis. A woman can talk on the phone while fixing dinner or arranging files, or redo her makeup while driving from appointment to appointment. But, many of these women who are adept at wearing many hats often find they are "out of balance." They are so busy doing what is urgent and immediate that they lose sight of what is important and eternal.

Some give up their dreams of personal achievement to raise a family. Others give up the joys of raising a family to pursue a career. Some work long hours at the office and at home with their family and have no time for their personal fitness or soul nurturing. A few women become so caught up in the breakneck pace of their lives that they lose all ability to laugh and have fun; they no longer find joy and wonder in their children, their spouse, their work, or themselves.

Let me be very clear here. Working hard to pursue a goal is worthwhile and important. The pursuit of a goal can teach perseverance and develop character, even as it brings rewards. But, when the pursuit of a goal overshadows the overall basics of a balanced life, problems *will* occur—perhaps not immediately, but certainly over time.

Take some time to reflect on the components of your life:

- Family
- Friends
- Work (even if you're a full-time homemaker)
- Spiritual Life
- Finances
- Physical Health
- Emotional Health
- Learning—a desire and need to improve and grow as a person

These eight basic components make up Life's Pie—indeed, "into eight pieces" is how most pies should be cut. Take a look at the chart below and then ask yourself: Which piece of pie do I wish I had more of right now? Generally, one or two pieces of this pie will come immediately to mind....

...I wish I was in better shape.

...I wish I was spending more time with my children or spouse.

...I miss times with my friends.

...I wish I had more time to read or take a course.

Life's Pie

In music, many children learn musical notation by two little phrases: F-A-C-E for the notes that go *between* the lines of a treble clef staff from bottom to top, and Every Good Boy Does Fine for the notes that go on the lines from bottom to top. For the eight pieces of your Life's Pie, I have devised this phrase:

Find What Satisfies Every Facet of Life
Fully and Peacefully!

The balanced life is a life of satisfaction and peace. It's your job to discover what is important to you in each of these areas. There's no one-size-fits-all formula. The test, however, for determining balance is the same:

- Do you feel deep inner peace and contentment—as if all is right with you personally even if everything is not all right in your immediate world or the world at large? Do you have PEACE?

- Do you have an abiding exhilaration that has you convinced that life is worth living for as long as possible with the greatest possible amount of quality? Do you have JOY?

- Do you have an abiding satisfaction that what you are doing is important and worthwhile? Do you have FULFILLMENT?

Different things bring feelings of peace, joy, and fulfillment to different people. For example, you may not WANT to wear a size four or have six children. You may not WANT a six-figure salary or have the desire to earn another academic degree. But in all likelihood you DO want to be healthy and have plenty of energy, have enough money to pay your bills, and find something that interests you and entices you to learn. In all likelihood you also want to have a relationship or some sort of link to the next generation. Identify precisely what fulfills *you* in each of these areas. Give yourself some time to reflect on how *you* define a balanced life.

One woman I know told me recently that she knows she's living a balanced life when she does these six things every day—and more precisely, first thing in the morning: spend some time in prayer and in reading inspirational material, go to a gym just two miles from her home to work out for thirty minutes, take vitamins along with a protein drink, do fifteen minutes' worth of needlework, practice the piano for a half hour, and write a few lines in a personal journal. "These six and I'm good," she said.

I admit I was a little surprised at the piano practice and needlework. She said, "The needlework clears my mind to think through the day, and it produces just a little bit of something that is likely to last a long time. Of all the things I do, the needlework I create is likely to survive the longest and continue to bring joy to my family and friends. The piano practice puts me in touch with something I did as a young person—I once played fairly well, and I'm relearning to play now. It's a mental exercise that is totally unlike my work."

"Doesn't it take a long time to get all these things done?"

"Well," she laughed, "it takes the first two hours of the day—from 6 a.m. to 8 a.m. Then I get dressed and head for the office with a very satisfied feeling that if I accomplish nothing else the rest of the day, I've done what is right for me over time."

"Explain that last part," I said.

"Exercise every day will produce better health over time," she said. "The same for the vitamins and protein drink. Nobody has perfect health, but I want to have the most energy and health I can have. Prayer and reading gives me spiritual energy and something positive to think about during the little interlude moments of life— from taking a shower to driving on the freeway. Over time, I grow spiritually. Piano practice is making me a slightly better pianist day by day. A little needlework every day eventually produces a finished gift item. All of these things are incremental. They are part of growth. If I *don't* do these things, I find that I have a nagging feeling that my life is just too busy, too stressful, too overly obligated. I feel stagnant."

"So these six things reflect a balanced life to you?" I asked.

"There are other things I need to do often, but not daily and certainly not first thing every morning. I need to connect with friends and family members and my godchildren with great frequency. I need to spend time with people who have the same values and faith that I have—usually two or three times a week. I need to go to a movie, play, theater performance, or gallery several times a month for creative input. All of these things help balance my tremendous drive to work—to produce, to create, to build. Work is very strong in my life and much of the rest is important to balance off work."

There are other women I know who have a very different mix of things that lead to a balanced life. One woman told me that she knows things are in balance if she and her family sit down to dinner three times a week and if they do something fun together as a family at least once a month. Another woman told me that she knows things are in balance if she has "after-work tea" with a friend at least once a week. Yet another woman told me that she needs to pay her bills once a week, go for a long drive with the top down on her convertible at least once a month, and have a "spa day" complete with pedicure and massage every six weeks.

What creates an inner sense of balance for you?

Are you *doing* the things you need to do with regularity?

What do you need to adjust in your life to bring about greater balance and an inner sense of fulfillment and peace?

The more you weave the various strands of your life into an overall pattern that is satisfying, joyful, and fulfilling to you, the more you are likely to stay on track and stay balanced.

Integrate Work and Relationships

There's a basic concept that seems especially important to women as they seek to create balance: Infuse your work with relationships.

Work ultimately is not all task or all people; it's a blend of both. One mark of success for women is finding a balance between

people and tasks. From my perspective, the best way to begin to find balance is to build your work around relationships. Keep relationships at the center. In very practical ways, this means including your family in as much of your work as possible. It also means developing friendships through work and in the workplace, and involving friends as much as possible in the work that you do.

Involve Your Family in Your Work. My first career was in music. As my children grew, so did my career. At the college where I was teaching I had a very flexible schedule, which I adjusted according to my children's needs. I taught piano and voice while they were in kindergarten or were taking naps. On weekends they went with me as I conducted concerts or directed theatre productions. As much as possible I integrated them into my activities.

As my children grew older they often took their homework with them as we traveled out of town. I arranged for baby-sitters in those cities where I was involved in business conventions. The children knew that at the end of the weekend, there would be a special treat for them—perhaps a trip to a zoo or a science museum in the city where we found ourselves. And of course, there was also a visit to their favorite fast-food restaurant.

Our life was a balancing act, but we were *together* in that balancing act. I knew where my children were; they were always close by. We used our travel time in the car for discussions about important issues and for storytelling. Sometimes we played tapes on a cassette player. We also played car games and learned things about the areas through which we were driving.

At times, when I had a business meeting at a restaurant, I'd set my children up in a nearby booth, talk to the waitress and tip her in advance, lay out the ground rules for my children (eat, and then do their homework), and say to them, "Don't make me come over here." I then felt free to conduct my business with a client over a nice dinner, and at the end of the evening, I'd celebrate the completion of my children's homework by buying them ice cream sundaes…with a cherry on top.

I learned a lot about this principle of integrating the family from my own family. As I mentioned earlier, when my father had a dairy, my sister and I had chores in that dairy. When my father was in the construction business, we had chores at his construction sites— everything from picking up lumber scraps and nails to sweeping finished-out rooms.

As I was growing up, I saw other people around me integrating family life and work. I had a wonderful role model in this with my aunt Ethel. In the late 1920s, her husband—my uncle Raymond— lost his job. Two of their children had died within a year of each other as a result of complications associated with measles. Left with only one child and a husband with no job, Aunt Ethel looked for solutions. Her sister had given her a piece of cloth to make a dress for my cousin. There was only one problem: Aunt Ethel had never sewn before. She decided she could learn to sew, however, and rather than make a dress for her own daughter, she decided to make a dress for a neighbor's daughter and see if she could make a little money.

She took the girl's measurements, drew a dress pattern on grocery sacks, and cut the cloth. She tried the dress on the child and found that it drooped on one shoulder. She took the dress apart and sewed it again. This time the hem was uneven. Again she took apart the dress and kept adjusting it until it fit perfectly. The neighbor woman was so pleased she agreed to pay Aunt Ethel fifty cents for the dress. Another neighbor saw the dress and asked Aunt Ethel to make *two* dresses for her daughter. She gave Aunt Ethel some money up front so she could purchase the fabric…and this was the launch of Aunt Ethel's business. Eventually, she had a multimillion-dollar dress-design business. She had two more children and in the end, my uncle and those two children were all part of the business—they could all sew, and at various times they made belts, turned sleeves, sorted buttons, and did whatever needed to be done. It was Uncle

Raymond's job to take the dresses to major department stores and obtain orders. It was a *family* business from the beginning.

Even if you don't set out to have a family-owned-and-operated business, your career *does* impact your family. Include your family members in your work life whenever and wherever appropriate.

Involve Your Friends. I know of a woman who once had a jam-making business. One of her good friends helped peel fruit. She later said, "My friend came over to help me with the ripened fruit for no salary—she said she came 'just so we could spend time together, talking and laughing.' We did a lot of both as we peeled and peeled. In the end, the jam-making business was only an average success, but the friendship was a tremendous success. I wouldn't trade her friendship today for anything."

Certainly I'm not advocating that you "use" your friends as free labor, but there are ways to integrate fun and work, friendships and responsibilities, family and chores. Be creative in this.

Many women I know were introduced to the idea of "mixing up their exercise routines"—or cross-training—through Jane Fonda aerobics tapes. We learned that it was good to change exercises from time to time—mix a little bicycle riding and swimming with walking or jogging. Different muscle groups need different exercises, and above all, the heart and lungs need to be exercised. Through the years, research has shown that women who add variety to their fitness activities tend to have a longer-lasting interest in exercise, exercise more regularly, and get more enjoyment out of exercise.

This concept of cross-training also works when it comes to involving your family and friends with the tasks of your work. And, it works in other areas of your life, such as your faith life or your social clubs. Let me give you just a few examples of how "tasks" and activities might be woven into your family life and friendships:

- Go on a fun faith-related retreat with your family and the families of friends.
- Exercise regularly with work associates.

- Form a reading club with friends at work for fun—but focus your reading on books related to the advancement of your career. Learn as you laugh, and laugh as you learn!
- Start a volunteer organization with friends who are part of your particular faith community.
- Participate in a coed softball team with people from your company.

You get the picture! Find ways to blend the various areas of your life together.

Process Is As Important As Product. With women, process is always more important than product. I have learned this through countless experiences in teaching women around the world to become financially independent. The methods of teaching the fundamentals of business in India are not the same as the methods of teaching business in Mexico. The "way" that I teach in South Africa is different from the methods I use in Sweden. But one thing is universal around the world: Women are PROCESS-oriented. They are relational. It doesn't matter if women come together from different backgrounds or face different challenges in their cultures—they want to connect with other women as friends. They want lasting relationships that are mutually satisfying, mutually rewarding, mutually encouraging.

I was recently in Hawaii with some business associates. We had several business meetings to attend. One evening one of my associates called me and said, "Let's order room service and eat in my room. I'll give you a pedicure." Wow, what an offer. I have since talked to friends who will have Girls Night Out and go to someone's house and do foot massages, pedicures, and manicures, and talk. What great therapy. And the price is right.

I have literally met thousands of people from around the world. Some of them have become my very good friends. We talk on the phone and write e-mails, we visit when we are in each other's respective countries, we enjoy cultural events like concerts and museums, and of course, we travel to exotic destinations together. There's nothing like sitting on a beautiful beach with your friends and family to make all the hard work worthwhile.

Balance Your Work and Non-Work Relationships

Again and again you are likely to come back to the truth: What really lasts in life? Relationships! Most of the *things* in our life are transient—we use them up, eat them up, wear them out, get tired of them and replace them, or in the case of houses, move from one to the next. Things tend to rust, rot, spoil, or decay. Relationships are what truly have a potential for *lasting*.

Don't allow yourself to become so result-oriented or task-oriented in your work that you lose sight of the importance of relationships with those who are NOT in your workplace. Allow others to share your joys, triumphs, sad times, and challenges—even as you seek ways to share in their joys, triumphs, sad times, and challenges.

The best way I know of to make relationships a priority is to make "develop and maintain good friendships" a life goal...and then, schedule time with your friends. If you don't schedule time for friends, you may very well find that weeks, even months, have gone by without a phone call or visit with a person you love. Be generous in including friends in social outings and events. Call a friend to meet for tea or dinner. Invite a friend to go to church with you and out to lunch later. If your friend lives far away, you may need to schedule visits by phone or periodic face-to-face visits in a mutually convenient location. To keep friendships alive, you must make time for friendships, and this often means balancing them against work commitments.

One of the things that most people intuitively know but seldom discuss is that it takes effort, sacrifice, and compromise to build a friendship or love a person. Make the effort! A new car, a designer wardrobe, a plaque on the wall, a top-floor corner office may make you feel good for a short time, but none of those things has the capacity to "love you back." Only a friend can do that.

Recognize, too, that your friends will know the instant in which you turn a friendship into a "task"—when you begin spending time with a person because you think you have to, or because you think it's important to your own advancement. Relationships are not "goals." They are a part of the ongoing ebb and flow of life. Relationships grow, change, and develop over time and over a multitude of experiences. Find things that are mutually enjoyable, such as eating dinner together, playing in a combo, singing in an ensemble group, or creating a book club. When people do tasks together, friendships grow naturally. When people create friendships solely for the purpose of using friends to generate income, friendships rarely survive, much less thrive.

It *is* possible to live a balanced life—one rich with both people and projects. It *is* possible to live a life that is structured, and yet within the broader structure, flexible and spontaneous. It *is* possible to live a life that is marked by pleasurable tasks and processes. It takes work to find the balance, but the end result is wonderful!

Create a Balanced Schedule According to Your Priorities

We all know what it means to have work deadlines. We often strive to meet those deadlines, and specific quotas or goals, at the expense of our personal needs for rest, relaxation, and time for creative input or creative expression. We often fail to eat properly or exercise sufficiently when we feel pressed to achieve work goals. Determine what is important to you and then SCHEDULE what is important into your life.

If eating dinner with your spouse and children is important to you, schedule your day to make that event happen. If exercising and having a quiet meditation time are important to you, write these activities into your schedule and keep those times as fixed appointments.

Many of the things that become urgent have reached "urgent" status only because we failed to plan ahead. Stop to think…to plan…to reflect and schedule. Take fifteen minutes at the beginning or end of a day to plan your next day's schedule. Take time once a week to anticipate what you need to do during the coming week, and map out a scheduling plan to avoid as many rush situations as possible.

Short bursts of goal-driven energy may be healthy and productive, but if you are constantly running, you will exhaust yourself. Focus on your most important goals and do those things FIRST.

Scheduling your priorities is especially important if you realize that one area of your Life's Pie is missing or undersized. For example, if you have had a major problem with your health, you'll need to spend ADDITIONAL time getting well and staying well. You may need to start an exercise plan, take a short course in good nutrition, and perhaps even spend some time at a spa to get your life back into balance. You may need to give up a bad health habit, such as drinking too much or smoking cigarettes. In the place of that bad habit, you need to establish a GOOD health habit—such as taking an afternoon walk around the block or working out at a gym three mornings a week. All of these things take time and intention; you will need to *schedule* health-related activities into your life, including extra sleep and recreation!

Let me ask you a few questions to help you begin to think of ways you may need to adjust your personal schedule for greater balance:

- Can you recall a meaningful family moment in the last week?

- When did you last help someone less fortunate than yourself, without using your checkbook to do so?

- What was the last spontaneous or even silly thing you did?

- When you hear the word "home," what comes to mind: chaos or comfort? What might you need to do to create more order, less clutter, greater harmony, and more peace?

- Have you spent any time recently indulging yourself without feeling guilty?

- Imagine yourself in twenty years looking back on your life today. Will you have regrets? What do you need to mark off of your schedule—or add to your schedule—so that you truly are living the fulfilling, meaningful, purposeful, joyful, and balanced life you want to live?

As you answer these questions, you may sense that there's a pattern or trend in your life that you dislike…or perhaps like. Spend some time thinking about that pattern or trend. Is there something you'd like to change, strengthen, renew, or work on?

DO Allow for Spontaneity. A word of caution as you "reschedule" your life: Don't schedule yourself so tightly that you have no room for spontaneity or flexibility. Treat interruptions as guests. They may be *unexpected* guests, but they can also be highly valuable guests. Great lessons learned and important personal relationships often begin with an unanticipated or unscheduled "encounter."

The act of balancing priorities is very often a balancing act between structure and spontaneity. To become too structured is to become rigid. To become too spontaneous is to become flighty and unfocused. Seek balance.

My daughter Debi learned a great lesson in this area. She once traveled to Europe with three of her university friends. The girls bought a train pass for two weeks of unlimited travel and before they left on their trip, they mapped out an itinerary. They decided to start their trip in Scandinavia and work their way down to Italy and Greece. On the very first day of the trip, they were unaccustomed to the twenty-four-hour clock that is used in

scheduling European trains (for example, twenty-two hundred hours is ten o'clock at night; eight hundred hours is eight o'clock in the morning). They missed their first train and felt as if they had spoiled their trip. Debi looked at the schedule and suggested they could still make an overnight train to Rome. Rather than end their trip in the southern nations of Europe, they spontaneously decided to *start* their trip there and work their way north. They had an amazing adventure as they rescheduled—yes, "restructured"—their trip along the way.

Be Quick to Recognize
When Things Are Out of Balance

Every driver I know seems to have experienced at least one flat tire. There's that first indication that the car just isn't handling right…there's an unusual thumping noise that captures attention…and then there's a brief moment of panic or frustration as you pull to the side of the road!

Most of us need to develop that same sense of awareness about "flat tires" in the broader scope of our lives. We need to be able to discern quickly when things are out of balance. An out-of-balance life is harmful; it adds stress and can leave you feeling physically and emotionally drained. An out-of-balance life, however, is not only harmful to you, it's harmful to your family and to other relationships you value.

Your children, especially, know when your life is out of balance. They may not be able to tell you in words, but they will tell you nonetheless as they act out their frustration and pain at what they perceive to be your absence or neglect of them. Certainly your spouse, your co-workers, and eventually your medical doctor may know when your life is out of balance.

Have you ever worked like a dog for two weeks straight so that when you finally got to a clear day on a weekend, you didn't want to move a muscle? Have you ever chased the children around the house to the point that you thought you were going crazy? We all overdo certain aspects of our lives from time to time, and we need to recognize that there's a point where we need to take a break…or things will begin to break down!

Now, I certainly recognize that there are seasons in life when one aspect of life can be all-consuming and very demanding. We all see that in our work lives. We all know that there are some weeks when all we seem to do is chauffeur children from event to event. In times of crisis or the death of a loved one, all of life can be consumed in dealing with the emergency or the grief. The goal of balance is to recognize quickly when we are overemphasizing one area of life to the detriment of other areas, and to take action sooner rather than later in order to restore balance.

Temporary exhaustion and burnout are two very different things. I travel a great deal. It is not uncommon for me to set foot in eight to ten nations in the course of a twelve-day business trip. On those trips, I know that as tired as I may get on the trip, when I return home, I will spend quality relaxation time with my family and friends. I also strive to find "hours of refreshment" along the way. Not long ago I was traveling in eastern Europe and when I reached Vienna I knew I needed a little "mini vacation." I had dinner at a lovely old castle and then went to a Viennese concert. Just those few hours of total relaxation and creative escape from work rejuvenated me so I could go on to Germany the next day feeling refreshed and ready to work. To another person, a night out of fine dining and fine music might have been a chore. For me, it was pure pleasure.

Discover and then DO what gives you a rejuvenating lift. Find what gives you creative input, food for your soul, and an emotional rest. Recognize that chemicals, whether alcohol or drugs, do not feed your creativity, your soul, or your body. They may offer an escape, but they do not truly rejuvenate and help restore balance. On the contrary, they create further imbalance. Do what is helpful to your whole being, never what is harmful.

Moving Toward Balance

Regaining balance oftentimes isn't as simple as giving more time to one area of Life's Pie that is missing or undersized. Regaining balance nearly always has an attitudinal or emotional component. Nearly every person I know needs to:

- *Laugh More.* Laughter is one of the greatest stress relievers. We need to learn to laugh in the workplace, laugh at the dinner table, and laugh as we drive to and from school, chauffeuring our children.

- *Listen and Observe More.* The two main senses through which we learn are sight and hearing. Listen to and look at the world around you. Take time to absorb the beauty you see and to take in ideas that are truly inspiring and uplifting.

- *Give and Receive More Hugs.* Reach out and touch other people. Give that pat on the back to a colleague. Put your arm around your child. Tuck your child into bed tonight with a kiss on the cheek—even if that child is an adult!

- *Praise Others More.* Offer genuine compliments and words of encouragement. They'll come back to you. Receive the compliments of others with gracious appreciation.

These attitudes can help bring greater emotional balance to ALL areas of your life!

Practice Session

1. Rate yourself on the scales below, with "1" as poor and "5" as excellent:

- I regard my friendships as "processes" rather than "projects."

$$1 \qquad 3 \qquad 5$$

- My life is balanced between work projects and people relationships.

1   3   5

- I have a good balance between giving myself creative "input" and engaging in work "output."

1   3   5

2. How do you feel about your responses to these statements? Is there something you want to change in your life?

How might you go about making that change?

Character

Building a Life on
Core Values

Who can find a virtuous woman? Her worth is far above rubies. She reaches out her hands to the needy. Her children rise up and call her blessed.

—KING SOLOMON

Neither praise nor money, the two powerful corrupters of mankind, seem to have depraved her [Mrs. Siddons].

—SAMUEL JOHNSON
WRITING IN *BOSWELL'S LIFE*, OCTOBER 1783

CHAPTER

In the operating room of a large, well-known hospital, a young nurse was completing her first day of full responsibility. "You've only removed eleven sponges, Doctor," she said to the surgeon she was assisting. "We used twelve."

"I removed them all," the surgeon declared. "We'll close the incision now."

"No," the nurse objected. "We used twelve sponges."

"I'll take the responsibility," the surgeon said sharply. "Suture!"

"You can't do that!" the nurse blazed back. "Think of the patient!"

The surgeon then smiled, lifted his foot, and showed the nurse the twelfth sponge. "You'll do," he said.

Now, that's the kind of nurse I want assisting on any surgery I might need to have!

Integrity means making a commitment to be consistent in what you believe in both your private and public life. It means speaking up in the face of a problem, even if speaking up involves a risk of ridicule or rejection. Your character is made strong when your values system is deeply rooted in principles that are both universal and lasting.

An Intensely Personal Decision

The morals, ethics, and values that you adopt *permanently* act as a rudder on the ship of your life, keeping you on course and balanced even when storms assail you. Selecting those principles by which you choose to live is an intensely personal decision. Unless the selection of your values is a personal choice, you will find that others around you will persuade you to compromise in ways that will leave you feeling hollow and guilty later on.

Ask yourself: "What are my values?"

Do you value money because it allows you to maintain a particular lifestyle?

Do you value time because it gives you freedom to be creative or to indulge in enjoyable activities?

Do you value other people because you receive energy, input, and love from them?

There are a million and one things you may or may not value. Determine what those things are.

Building a Life on Values

How can you build a life on values? First, you must decide what you hold to be the universal truths of life. By universal truths, I mean absolutes.

We live in an age, of course, in which the word "absolute" tends to be in absolute disfavor! People today want relative truth—your truth is your truth, my truth is my truth. People often say they want to live in a world in which every person is able to live by his or her own set of values and still find a way to live in peace with everybody. *It isn't possible!* The only way we truly can live in peace and harmony with other people is if we agree upon absolute, universal principles. The absolute truth functions as the third point in a triangle: You believe the absolute truth, I believe the absolute truth, and together, we find common ground for agreeing on how to proceed on tasks and build a solid relationship.

It defies all logic to deny the existence of absolute truths and universal principles regarding human affairs. From centuries past, we have thousands upon thousands of recorded examples that make one thing perfectly clear: Some aspects of human nature are unchanging and "affixed" to the very definition of what it means to be a human being.

Just as physical laws govern the physical universe, so universal principles govern human existence. If these laws are violated, the consequences are predictable. If a person steps off the roof of a ten-story building, gravity kicks in and the person plummets to the ground below…whether the person "believes" this will happen or not. In like manner, if a person violates a basic law of human nature, the consequences are inevitable. It doesn't matter if we understand that law of human nature or "buy into it." The principles function with as much predictability as natural law.

A major goal in our pursuit of potential, therefore, becomes that goal of discovering and applying absolute and universal principles. For many people, that process involves acquiring *wisdom*. The word "wisdom" in the Hebrew language has an interesting connotation. It refers to "craftsmanship." To be wise is to be a craftsman at living—an artisan of life. I like that approach! I want to be an artisan of life…always moving my life and managing it in such a way that I find balance, harmony, meaning, satisfaction, beauty, and fulfillment.

I want to find those principles of life that allow me to experience inner balance and outer significance.

I want to have the greatest possible impact for good in the lives of my family members, friends, and community.

Developing Strong Character

Many people refer to the central core of a person's beliefs as character. Issues of character and integrity seem to be at the forefront of the corporate culture these days. Employers routinely state that after skills, they are most interested in an employee's character, specifically his or her trustworthiness, loyalty, and work ethic.

There's also a growing recognition that many of the popular diversions in our culture assault character. Video games, movies, television programs, and many Internet sites promote values or include situations that are the very opposite of what the majority of our society's members define as "good morals." Character and integrity need to be guarded carefully. The values that we hold dear need to be nurtured and strengthened, not demeaned or subjected to ridicule.

How does a person develop character? There are several aspects to character development.

To build a strong central core of beliefs, however, a person first needs to be able to differentiate between personality and character. Personality has to do with attributes that attract or repel others—a winning smile, a sparkling wit, candor, good communication skills, and a person's set of likes and dislikes. Character, by contrast, has to do with traits such as kindness, gentleness, a willingness to serve others, caring concern, integrity, honesty, a desire to promote goodness, and loyalty. Character traits are all rooted in a person's "being," not in their circumstances. These traits apply whether a person owns a lot or a little, or whether a person is educated or uneducated, is socially sophisticated or unsophisticated, or has a sparkling or bland personality. Character traits span cultural upbringing, race, age, and sex.

At the heart of character is integrity—saying what you mean or believe, doing what you say, and speaking and acting with consistency over time, in all situations and relationships.

There is a great little book by Dr. Gregory Stock called *The Book of Questions*. In it are more than two hundred questions about integrity—such as, "What would you do for money?" and "How do you view life?" It is an excellent book to read with your spouse or a good friend because it makes you think and articulate your principles and deeply held beliefs.

Stop for a minute and ponder what basic life principles are most important to you. On what tenets are you not willing to compromise? Look at the principles that govern you at work, home, in your spiritual life, and in your friendships. Try to identify how you operate in each of those spheres of influence. Do you apply different principles in different areas? Or do you hold fast to one set of principles in all areas of your life?

Conduct a Values Audit

To determine what your values really are, use these four methods:

- **First,** take a look at your calendar. How do you spend your discretionary time? How do you set priorities when deciding how to use your time? What you take time to do is what you value!

- **Second,** take a look at your checkbook. What are you buying with your discretionary money? How do you set

priorities in your spending? What you spend money on is what you value!

- **Third,** take a look at what it is you tend to think about the most— especially your first thought in the morning and your last thought before falling asleep.

- **Fourth,** spend a little time reflecting on who you consider your personal heroes to be. What is it about their lives that you admire? Whom do you desire to emulate?

I encourage you to make a one-week log of your life. Record all your activities; this will show you how you *truly* spend your time. Record your expenses. Make notes about what you dream about and the people you most admire. Stop several times a day to record your observations. At the end of the week, spend an hour or two reflecting on what you have written. Then ask yourself these key questions:

- Are these the things I truly VALUE, or have I just fallen into bad habits?

- If these activities, ideas, expenses, and people are not reflecting the values I want in my life, what changes do I need to make?

Discovering what truly is important to you can be an eye-opening experience.

Several years ago my daughter Debi learned this firsthand. She had just graduated from college. She had her own apartment and had strong ideas and opinions about how she wanted to live her life and forge her future. She had a good job and lots of friends.

This was the first time Debi had been totally out on her own. She realized that in the eyes of everyone around her, she was an adult and she could choose what she would do with her time and energy. In other words, she could choose what kinds of books to read, music to listen to, TV shows to watch, and so forth. There were no parents, no professors, and no peers to pressure her into making these choices. She felt liberated!

A few weeks later as she reflected upon her independence, Debi decided that she had been going to the movie theater in a mindless manner. Since movie-going had always been a social activity for her, she had gone to see movies in recent weeks without asking too much about each movie's message. She realized that she had been bombarded mentally with a significant number of stories that were about adultery, lying, cheating, thievery, abuse, murder, rape, and other forms of violence. As Debi became aware of this, she said to herself, "These aren't my values!" Immediately, she made a quality decision that she would not see a movie unless it had an uplifting, moral message.

Debi missed out on some social outings, and she later admitted she missed the "movie event of the decade," but at the same time, she felt good about her decision and gained a new awareness that she was making a conscious decision about what she was putting into her own mind.

Today, Debi goes to the occasional movie, especially comedies, but she makes deliberate choices about what she sees. She continues to seek to put *into* her mind and heart what she wants to flow *out* of her mind and heart.

What about you?

Refuse to Blur Right and Wrong

One of the greatest temptations we each face is the temptation to conclude that a particular law, rule, or standard doesn't apply to us for some reason. People routinely seem to assume that a particular principle doesn't impact their life because they are of a particular social class, religious upbringing, racial or ethnic background, or because they have become more sophisticated, educated, or have risen to a high level of power. The truth is, moral principles are moral principles—right and wrong do not change because circumstances change. Neither is there one set of right-and-wrong standards for one group of people, and a different set of right-and-wrong standards for another group.

A couple of years ago I read about a woman in the state of Washington who had pleaded guilty to embezzling more than thirty-one thousand dollars from a local youth soccer club. The money had been raised through registration fees and candy sales. This woman reportedly saw no problem in "borrowing" from this fund to buy shoes, vacation trips, and even a new car! After all, she reasoned, she was the treasurer—as if being the treasurer meant the money was hers!

People continually justify and find excuses for all kinds of behavior. It's easy to do.

Failing to tell a spouse about a dress that was purchased and lying about the discrepancy in the checkbook...

Taking office supplies for personal use at home...

Spending office hours on personal business...

Cheating on taxes...

Lying to a credit-card company about whether a check has been sent...

Behaviors such as these seem to be second nature for some people. I strongly encourage you not to be such a person!

When we begin to allow these lines of right and wrong to blur, we will find it very difficult to chart a clear course toward our potential. We must be able to discern between true and false, authentic and counterfeit, and lasting principles and fleeting fads.

Go Back to the Basics

"But how," you may be asking, "can I tell right from wrong?"

In my experience, I have found that the vast majority of people know if something is right or wrong. They ask a question such as this because they are looking for a loophole for justifying a particular behavior they find pleasurable or personally gratifying!

If you have any questions, go back to what you learned from your grandparents, or from the person who gave you religious instruction as a child (such as a Sunday school teacher).

You may be saying, "But if I hold to strict principles, won't I become rigid and intolerant?"

No! A thousand times, no! You will become confident, stable, and focused. You will find yourself feeling grounded and anchored, and as a result, be in a position to make far wiser choices and decisions.

In many ways, your various acts of behavior are like petals on the flower of your life. They are visible and obvious to those around you. Your core values and principles are unseen; they are like the roots that anchor you to the ground. You may have deep, healthy roots...or shallow ones. The deeper your roots, the more resilient you are.

Furthermore, there's nothing automatically intolerant about living your life according to a code of values based upon universal, absolute principles—especially not if one of those principles is, "Love your neighbor as yourself"!

Forgive and Move Forward

What do we do when others violate our values or cast aspersions on our character?

What do we do when we personally fail to live up to our own values?

We must forgive.

Many people have an inaccurate definition of what it means to forgive. Forgiveness does not mean that we deny the hurt we have felt or deny the fact that we have been injured. Forgiveness does not sweep the incident or experience under the rug and say, "It didn't really matter." Forgiveness, rather, is a willful choice to *refuse* to hold onto the hurt or to keep the person locked up in our own vengeful heart. Forgiveness is "letting go" of the person emotionally.

Many times, the foremost person we need to forgive is our own self. We need to "let go" of what we have done, refusing to rehearse it or relive the memories of it any longer. We need to admit our sorrow over our misdeed or failure, openly acknowledge and express a desire to live in a different way, and then move forward with confidence and a head held high.

None of us is ever going to live a one-hundred-percent perfect life when it comes to lining ourselves up with absolute and universal moral principles. We will all fail on this score. But the answer is not to give up on values; it's to seek forgiveness for our moral failures. As a part of that forgiveness process, we need to ask forgiveness of others we have hurt. We need to make whatever apologies or amends are most beneficial to the other person. Once that is done, we need to move forward with new resolve that we are going to live *according to* our principles and values, not *in spite of* our principles and values.

I learned this in a time of pain. I made a choice to divorce my husband and marry another man. What a disastrous decision that turned out to be! Within months I realized what an awful mistake I had made and I obtained yet another divorce. The process was long and difficult, and in the end, I was once again on my own.

After months of counseling, as well as talking to my children and asking for their forgiveness, and for the forgiveness of others, I began to make new associations and create a different life for myself. I read a number of books about people who overcame struggles and who had made mistakes and survived. I made friends with people who were living the kind of life I admired and sought to have.

Through my own experience in this hard school of personal pain, I have become convinced that in ninety-nine-point-nine percent of all cases, it is possible to recover fully from a bad choice, moral failure, or poor decision. It is possible to be forgiven and to forgive. I will be forever grateful to those who stood with me during the difficult times in my life—those who prayed for and with me, listened to me, cried with me, and helped me through. The tragedy of moral failure is not that we experience the moral failure; the real tragedy is when we don't know we have failed, don't care that we have failed, or don't seek to change our attitudes, beliefs, commitments, and behavior so we can morally *succeed*!

No matter what you may have done in the past, you *can* move forward today. Call to mind the principles that you KNOW are right and make a decision that you WILL live by them.

One of the most amazing turnaround stories I've witnessed in recent years is that of tennis star Jennifer Capriati. At age fourteen, she had won major tournaments and was making millions in endorsements. Within three years, however, she had hit bottom. She was picked up for shoplifting a three-dollar ring at a mall, was busted in a seedy motel room for possession of marijuana, and then went through rehab. Most people thought her tennis career was all but finished before she was even old enough to vote.

After several years of being away from the game, Capriati staged a comeback. She was starting from a position of low self-esteem and no wins. She felt heat from all sides as critics, coaches, players, and fans all voiced opinions about her past behavior and some poor performances. There were times, Capriati has said, when she felt like quitting the game for good. But, she didn't. She continued to work on her game, set aside the negative comments leveled at her, and reshaped both her game and her *self*. She began an intensive regimen of exercise in the off-season—swimming, running, lifting weights, and hitting ball after ball on the court. At age twenty-five, Jennifer Capriati emerged on the world stage as a new player, and a new person. Gone were the feelings of insecurity and doubt. Gone were the headline-attracting personal mistakes. She started winning and winning big. Two Grand Slam victories and an amazing showing at Wimbledon secured her position as a player who had "come back to success."

Her story can be *your* story.

There are four questions I encourage you to ask as you go through the next few weeks:

1. Do I schedule time for activities that reflect my most basic values and principles?

2. Do I keep my schedule as I planned? In other words, do I actually engage in activities I know are in keeping with my values and principles?

3. How do I spend my idle time? Do I interpret "time off" as being time when I don't have to be "good" or don't have

to continue to live up to the moral excellence I desire as a trait of my life?

4. Do other people see my behaviors as matching up to what I proclaim to believe or to hold as values?

This last question calls a person to accountability. For you to know how others see you, you must be in relationship with people you trust to tell you the truth about yourself. Do you have a friend who will say to you, "Hey, you're better than that!" or, "You don't really believe that's the right thing to do, do you?"

Talk about Your Values

There's an old saying that people with little minds talk about other people and activities. People with great minds talk about ideas and values.

Choose to become a person who talks about what you *believe*. Two things will happen:

First, the more you talk about your beliefs and principles, the more confirmed you will become in your own thinking and feeling about what it is that you truly believe and hold to be absolute truth. Very often it is as we speak about universal and absolute principles that we remind ourselves of what it is that we consider to be the "highest" ideal or the "right" way to live.

Second, the more you are willing to talk about your beliefs and principles, the more you will attract people to you who are of like mind and heart. It is far easier to live up to your ideals when you are surrounded by friends and associates who also have high moral standards and who are seeking to live an ethical, right-thinking life.

Just as you attract others to you who are of high moral character, you are likely to make it uncomfortable for people of low character to be in your presence. That isn't bad. In fact, it's good!

People will be far less likely to tell you dirty jokes, use crude, lewd, or foul language in your presence, or invite you to participate in activities that are morally wrong. Women, especially, find that if they are willing to speak up about their values, men respect them more. There are far fewer instances of date rape and abuse in relationships where women are quick to speak about their values and to make choices that reflect those values.

A man on an airplane once leaned over to me about halfway through the flight and said, "You know what? I've spent the last hour trying to hit on you and you are the most professional woman I have ever met. You ignored what I was doing entirely." I said, "That was on purpose."

I don't change my tone of voice or treat any incident as though it bothers me or makes me uneasy. I choose to remain matter-of-fact and kind. I continue to use my womanly intuition, express feelings, make eye contact, and use appropriate body language...but I do *not* use sex appeal in my business dealings or casual conversations. Around the world, I have found that it is very possible to be direct, honest, personal, and to communicate openly—without having to compromise any of the moral values that I know are right.

Personal potential-reaching success, in the end, doesn't mean a thing if it isn't grounded in values. And values aren't worth much if they aren't the highest and best values that are universal and absolute.

Practice Session

1. Clarify your values by responding to each of the questions below with several words or phrases:
   - How do I tend to spend my discretionary (non-work, non-family-obligated) time?

· How do I tend to spend my discretionary money (after fixed bills)?

· Who are my heroes?

· What do I often find myself thinking about?

2. List five principles that you would like to guide your life: (I hope "Always tell the truth" is one of them!)

1) _____

2) _____

3) _____

4) _____

5) _____

3. What are the values that you most want to be remembered for by your children (or if you don't have children, by young people who may be observing your life)?

Destiny

Embracing a Personal Life Mission

The heights by great men reached and kept
Were not attained by sudden flight,
But they, while their companions slept,
Were toiling upward in the night.

—LONGFELLOW
(FROM "THE LADDER OF SAINT AUGUSTINE")

As the mother of an elementary school child, Janice Lind was always concerned about how her son fit in at school. She only wanted the best for him so when he said he was going to try out for the school play, she was concerned. She knew his heart was set on getting a part and she worried that he would not be chosen. On the day the parts were awarded, Janice went to pick up her son at school. He rushed to the car, his eyes shining with pride and excitement. "Guess what, Mom?" he shouted. "I've been chosen to clap and cheer!"

Oh, the simple desires of children! That little boy didn't believe he had to get the lead to be a success. He just wanted a part and his place in the play.

And isn't that what we all want? We all want a part in life's play…in history's play…a part in the unfolding of the great human drama. We all want to believe that our lives have made a difference and that we have not lived in vain.

I was in Cape Town, South Africa, on a business trip when I heard that Princess Diana had been in a tragic automobile accident. All through the long night the world watched and prayed that her life might be spared. Questions were voiced and left unvoiced by millions upon millions of people around the world: How could such a thing happen? Why does it seem the good die young? What will happen to her children? Was sabotage involved?

Her death seemed such a tragic end to a life that had been marked by much sorrow, and yet, by such a willingness to help so many.

The next morning my friends drove me by the home of Diana's brother, Earl Spencer, located just outside Cape Town. Already there were flowers and remembrances positioned at the home's entrance in memory of his famous sister.

A few days later I flew to London. I was not at all prepared for the tremendous grief being expressed by the people there. My friend, Derek Lawrence, is a London taxi driver. He picked me up at Heathrow Airport and immediately he drove me to Harrods so I might sign the guest book of those who wished to pay their respects to the families of Diana and the man with whom she was riding in the car at the time of her death. Up and down the street I saw flowers, gifts, and notes piled high. We then drove to Buckingham Palace. The last two blocks leading up to the palace entrance were also piled high with flowers, gifts, and notes. Thousands of people lined the streets.

The most amazing sign of respect that I experienced was the *silence* of the city. There were no horns honking, no people talking, no bells ringing…only silence. The entire city seemed to stand still in shocked bereavement.

Derek took me to a flower shop where I bought a dozen long-stemmed white roses to take to Westminster Abbey. As I stood outside the cathedral, I saw not only crowds of people but thousands of bouquets already there. The funeral was scheduled for the next day and already, the Abbey was closed and the media was in position. I stood at the edge of the large crowd holding my flowers when a rector at the Abbey came to me and asked if he could help me. I told him I had a very special request. Inside the nave was the tomb of a woman who had been buried there out of respect for all her work for the poor. I asked him if he would lay my flowers in front of that tomb, knowing that Diana's body would also pass by that location. He bowed his head and said he would be happy to honor my request—he knew just the tomb I meant.

I have returned to Westminster Abbey on a number of occasions and have stood in front of that tomb where I had asked that my flowers be laid. I have thought about the impact of the woman buried there, as well as the impact made by Princess Diana and other women of great distinction and legacy who had a personal mission for helping the poor, the disenfranchised, and the helpless.

These were women who left a legacy of significance. I am determined that my life will not just be successful, but also significant in some way. Certainly I don't expect my life to be marked in the grand way these women have been honored, but I

do want my children to remember me as a person who always helped those less fortunate. Every woman can leave that kind of legacy.

Discovering Your Mission

Women today seem to be pulled in a hundred directions at once. We all wear many hats during the course of any given day. Bosses, friends, children, spouses, clients, customers, vendors—all seem to vie for our undivided attention. It can be difficult at times to know just how to manage a day. At times it is impossible.

One of the things that can help tremendously in ordering a day, and ultimately in ordering a life, is to focus on what you see as your life's "mission." Ask yourself this key question:

*What is the big-picture plan for what I hope
to do and leave behind?*

The more you can clarify and define your answers to that question, the easier it will be to build purpose and meaning into *everything* you do.

Carrie Schwab Pomerantz is a wife, mother, and mentor to young women. She is also the creator of Women Investing Now (WIN) at the brokerage firm of Charles Schwab. Pomerantz has a mission in life to help women and girls achieve financial security.

Pomerantz, as you may have guessed, is the daughter of Charles Schwab. She was a young girl when her parents divorced and she learned firsthand that life doesn't always go the way you want it to go. She realized that she needed to have a game plan for her life, and part of that game plan was a need to become financially savvy. She sees that need as being common to all women.

Several years ago Pomerantz approached her father about developing an investment program specifically aimed at women. She especially wanted to target women who suddenly found themselves single, either through divorce or the death of a spouse. Pomerantz did her research and found that about ninety percent of women will find themselves in a position of being solely responsible for their finances at some point in their lifetime. Only about ten percent of these women, however, have experience in investing when that time comes.

Pomerantz developed WIN into a successful program for women of all ages and all walks of life. She has a clearly defined mission and because she does, the way in which she manages her professional and personal time has a specific framework. She is able to ask about every key meeting, decision, or choice, "Does this further my mission or detract from it?"[1]

Women who are intent upon fulfilling their potential nearly always have a well-defined understanding of their *purpose* in life. As a result, they accomplish much more in their lives than those women who are less concerned about purpose or who have not yet developed their own unique "mission statement."

Certainly not all mission statements need to be focused on business goals. Some may be philanthropic. Some may involve personal goals. Some may be spiritual. Whatever your mission statement may have as its focus, a mission statement should inspire—yes, COMPEL you to move forward to your destiny.

Sarah was a young woman born with a muscle missing in her foot. At age ten, she wore a brace. One spring day she came home from school to tell her father that she had competed in a "field day," which was a day filled with running races and competitions in other aspects of track and field. As Sarah told her father about the day, his mind turned to the encouraging words he might give to his daughter because he felt certain she must be discouraged. To his surprise, she announced, "Daddy, I won two of the races!" Then she added, "I had an advantage, though." Her father sighed, thinking his daughter must have been given a head start. Before he could respond, she said, "My advantage was that I had to try harder."

A mission in life pushes you to try harder. It motivates you to give your best.

The Power of
Having a Mission

Fear is a major element that keeps many women from pursuing or achieving their potential. Some women don't believe they have anything to contribute to the world. Others don't want to take a risk or a leap of faith. Still others don't know how or when to get started. A mission statement can help a woman overcome the obstacles of fear, lack of self-value, reluctance, and indecision.

Katherine Graham was the publisher of *The Washington Post* for more than thirty years. She came to that position after her husband, the owner of The Washington Post Company, died. Prior to her husband's death, Graham was known as a socialite and housewife. By the time she died, she was hailed as one of America's foremost leaders in journalism and business.

Katherine Graham was forty-six years old when she became the publisher of the Post. At the beginning, she didn't feel at all adequate for the job. She later said, "What I essentially did was to put one foot in front of the other, shut my eyes, and step off the ledge. The surprise was that I landed on my feet." Graham had been so shy that she practiced saying "Merry Christmas" before she went to the company's first holiday party in her position as owner. Ten years later she impacted the course of our national history in the decisions she made about publishing the Pentagon Papers and pursuing the Watergate story.

Katherine Graham had a mission: to be "complete, accurate, fair, and as excellent as possible." She succeeded…genuinely.[2]

Your mission statement can be whatever you choose. It can be directed toward a particular task, or toward a particular set of ideals. Above all, it needs to flow from your deepest desires and interests. Your mission statement should be as unique as *YOU* are.

I strongly encourage you to write down your mission statement. Putting it in writing helps you clarify it. It also helps you remember it and keep it at the forefront of your thinking.

Framing Your Mission Statement

How might you get started in framing such a statement?

- **First,** focus on your unique gifts and talents and grapple with the question,"Why do I exist?"This is a heavy question, one that takes deep thought and prayer. Set aside some quiet, quality time to consider your answer. Be honest with yourself. Your mission statement needs to flow out of the gifts, talents, and desires that you already have.

- **Second,** reexamine the core principles and values that you identified in the previous chapter. Your mission statement must be totally in sync with those values.

- **Third,** an extremely important step is this: Ask yourself, "What difference can I make in the world around me?"

   Don't feel as if you need to take on the whole world at this point in your life. Focus on what you can do to help a specific person or group of people who are already in your sphere of influence and acquaintance. These people may be your neighbors, the homeless who are coming to your church for food or clothes, the children your son or daughter plays with, a "problem child" or a "hurting family" that lives in your apartment complex, the school down the street that is underfunded, the city library project that is about to be canceled, and so forth.

   The NEED that you identify should be one that you have either the interest or the skill to address. Notice that word "or" in the previous sentence. At times, our skills draw us toward specific problems or needs because we have confidence that we know what to do or can help in resolving a difficulty. At other times, our hearts draw us toward specific people—we may not feel we have the skills necessary, but we have a voice and hands, and a heart that is deeply interested in getting involved and making a difference.

- **Fourth**, a mission statement should be one with fairly obvious implications for every slice of your Life's Pie:

  1. **Family.** A mission statement needs to take into consideration the role you have with your family. A mission statement should never bypass family, or supersede family. Rather, a personal mission statement should automatically extend with harmony to *include* all family members.

  2. **Work.** Whether you are a stay-at-home mom or the president of a Fortune 500 company, your business or career may be the *means* through which you accomplish much or all of your mission statement.

  3. **Spiritual Life.** Your mission statement is likely very closely aligned with your spiritual life. It should be in complete harmony with your deeply held religious convictions and spiritual values.

  4. **Emotional Health.** While a mission statement is serious, it should also be the most exhilarating undertaking of your life. You should feel energized and enriched by what you intend to pursue and accomplish. There should be a strong "this is pure fun" streak running through your mission statement. I know one woman who says she grins every time she reads the mission statement she has written on the opening page of her personal journal. She says, "I can hardly believe I GET to do this in my life and with my life. I wake up every morning excited about what aspect of my mission I might tackle and accomplish that day." Ultimately, your mission statement should give you a strong sense of inner peace, as if this is what you were created to do and be...this is what will fulfill you completely...this is what will satisfy your longing for a purpose-driven life.

5. **Friendships.** A mission statement may limit friendships, and it may push you in the direction of forming some new friendships, but in the long run, a mission statement should be one that allows you to have deep and meaningful friendships with people who hold like values and who appreciate and applaud the purpose that you have adopted for your life. Friends are especially important to women—don't discount their role in your life. You need people in whom you can confide and with whom you can talk about those aspects of your life that are distinctly female.

6. **Learning.** Your mission statement should build upon what you already know and have experienced, but also challenge you to learn something new—about yourself, about other people, about the world as a whole.

7. **Finances.** A mission statement always has a financial dimension, even if that isn't mentioned in the formal statement. If you have a goal, it's going to cost you something to pursue, develop, and implement that goal. The fulfillment of a mission statement ultimately requires that you have a healthy and balanced approach to dealing with money, retirement funds, college savings, and taxes. The dollar figures aren't all that's important— your perspective on and attitude toward money are of the utmost importance.

8. **Physical Health.** Your mission statement should do nothing to detract from (in fact, it should enhance) your pursuit of physical health. It should compel you to explore new ideas and to undertake new disciplines so you can accomplish the most you can accomplish during a long life marked by high "quality of living." I heard a woman say recently, "I don't know how long I'll live; that's not my decision. But I do know how WELL I want to live;

that's a decision I'm mostly responsible for making. I want to be healthy, with lots of loving relationships with family members and friends, have financial security, and be involved in giving myself away at every turn. I'm the one responsible for putting into place what will give me this quality of life twenty years from now." This woman wants to be well physically, emotionally, financially, and have significance. That's "fitness"!

- **Fifth,** within each piece of Life's Pie, develop a balance between output and input, and between serious expenditure of thought and energy and "fun" times of recreation. No matter how hard you work and no matter how tightly you schedule yourself toward the mission you intend to fulfill, you also need to take time for some crazy, spontaneous things that keep your life creative, unique, and memorable. Planning for fun and creative input within the pursuit of your mission is a way of relieving stress, strengthening your relationships with others who are helping you accomplish your mission, and enjoying the PROCESS of the mission as much as the accomplishment of the mission.

Take Into Consideration Your Past

In many ways, your past has formed who you are today. Don't discount your past in planning your future. You may not want or need to have your past DICTATE your future, but you certainly should consider the positive and constructive aspects of your past as you form your mission statement.

When I first developed my mission statement I took time to reflect on my life, my history, and my family upbringing. I used all of my life experience to fashion a mission that is unique to me. Remembering certain aspects of my childhood helped me construct a statement with which I could truly "connect" my various interests and desires.

When I was growing up my mother sewed most of the clothes my sister and I wore. We went to a large church where my parents had many friends, and it seemed about once a year my sister and I would be asked to be candle lighters in a wedding because we were both tall, about the same height, and many people thought we were twins. My mother would sew our dresses, often taffeta ones that swished as we walked down the aisle to light the darkened church with our glowing candle torches. As young girls we found this very exciting. It was one of our favorite activities.

For me, being a "candle lighter" is still my favorite thing to do. My mission is to lighten the dark corners of the world where I travel and to give people hope for a better life. I believe that if I can bring light into another person's life by way of words, a smile, or a good business opportunity, I will help that person and at the same time, feel fulfilled. I have absolutely no doubt that encouragement is one of the most important gifts that can be given to a person. I want to be a person who lavishes encouragement on others.

Candles are often blown out by winds of adversity, discouragement, doubt, and depression. Part of my mission is to go out and help others RELIGHT their candles. Elisabeth Elliot once said, "If I can light another's candle, it doesn't take away from the glow of mine." That's how I choose to live—sharing light with others.

Is this a mission that energizes me? Absolutely.

Does it give me a sense of purpose, direction, and focus for every encounter I have in any given day? Certainly!

Does it make me feel a glow of satisfaction at the end of a day? Yes…a thousand times, yes.

Heather Reynolds grew up wanting to run an orphanage. Her parents were traders in the Transkei in South Africa and she loved growing up with the rural children of that area. As she got older her family discouraged her dream. She trained to become a nurse but found she couldn't cope with the death and grief that are frequently a part of the nursing profession. She changed careers and worked for an insurance company. She found herself becoming more and more disillusioned with the world.

One day as Heather was traveling home from picking up her baby son after a meeting, the brakes on her car went out and she went speeding through a busy intersection. Almost instantly she was hit by another car. Her baby son was thrown under the seat but was unharmed. Heather looked up and saw that the car with which she had collided was a brand-new Jaguar sports car. Shaken but unhurt, Heather got out of her car expecting to receive strong verbal abuse from the man driving the other vehicle. Instead, he asked her if she was all right and then he began to pray, thanking God that both of them were safe and unharmed.

Soon after the accident Heather and her husband, Patrick, decided to move to a farm in rural South Africa. Not long after their move, Heather and Patrick found themselves taking care of a fourteen-year-old girl who was pregnant and had lost her family in the racial violence that spread across South Africa in the early 1980s. It was highly unusual for a white family to take in a black girl, but they didn't have the heart to turn their backs on her.

Shunned by her neighbors and family, Heather continued to help young pregnant girls that showed up on her doorstep. She took care of their children while they finished school and she helped the girls raise money so they could start a pottery business for bonsai trees. "I knew nothing about pots," Heather later said, but she and her girls soon became one of the nation's largest suppliers of potted bonsai.

Eventually Heather and her husband found themselves housing thirty-eight refugees of the racial violence. They needed more funds to help house and feed these "visitors." Heather's sister heard of a particular business opportunity in a neighboring nation, and she suggested that Heather try selling asphalt mixing trucks to the Ugandan government. One sale could help her start up a small business project, so Heather agreed to give it a try.

On her first plane trip to Uganda, Heather found herself sitting next to the wife of a Ugandan parliament member. Within hours of landing she had an audience with the Minister of Transport and she sold her first piece of equipment. The transaction happened so fast that Heather found herself with some free time. She hired a vehicle to take her around the countryside where she saw groups of children suffering from AIDS. Many of them were orphans. Heather's heart broke as she saw them wandering about without adults to look after them. She said, "I made a commitment at that moment to spend the rest of my life helping children like these."

Back at home, Heather saw a program about the AIDS orphans in her own nation of South Africa. She called the physician she saw on the program and told him she wanted to help. The physician suggested she try to start a foster-care center.

Heather's vision ultimately included having a self-sufficient enterprise that encompassed an art gallery, crafts center, playground, and swimming pool for the children. She found an abandoned resort that she purchased to start her orphanage. Today the center is bustling with orphans, some of whom have AIDS. The orphanage has a school and a training center that teaches youths from the community how to make bricks for construction projects. By the way—you may have seen footage of Heather and some of these facilities on a television special about Oprah Winfrey's trip to Africa.

When the center's chairman recently stepped down from his position, one of the other board members recommended a man named Alan McCarthy for the chairman's role. McCarthy, the chairman of a group called African Enterprise, had a high profile in South Africa, a factor that would be beneficial in helping the center grow. Alan McCarthy also turned out to be the man who had prayed with Heather so many years before when she had collided with his Jaguar sports car![3]

Ultimately, your mission in life will give you a sense that a number of aspects of your life are finally pulled together. There should be a sense of destiny about your mission—a feeling that you were born for this, that you were always being prepared for this, that you were "designed" and "directed" all through your life to accomplish this mission.

A genuine heartfelt mission statement both establishes you and points you toward challenges. It can give you stability when you encounter obstacles. It can also give you perspective and renewed motivation in times of discouragement.

Women who are in hot pursuit of their potential don't wait for the world to come knocking on their doors. Instead, they chase after their goals and dreams. They MAKE things happen.

Embracing a Mission that Has Been "Predetermined" for You

There are times when a person finds herself in a position that seems to have been "predetermined." Sometimes this predetermination is from birth. Sometimes it is the result of a relationship choice. For example, you may not be able to help the fact that you were born into a family with an expectation that you would one day take over the family business. But, if you marry a missionary, you can expect to be on the mission field. If you marry a politician, you can expect to be in the limelight.

When the predetermination is a matter of inheritance—perhaps of money, perhaps of title—a woman has a choice: Will she embrace the role of managing and maintaining…increasing actively…or simply spending her estate? Whatever she chooses—and I personally would hope that her choice would be to increase it and spend it on philanthropic enterprises—she has a "mission in life" that was not of her direct choosing. The same is true for a woman who finds herself born into royalty.

Rania Al-Yasin is a woman who embraced a destiny that was somewhat determined for her. Born into a Palestinian refugee family, she is a beautiful woman who attended American University in Cairo and graduated with a degree in Business Administration. After graduation she took a job as a banker and when she was twenty-two years old, she married. One year later she had her first child. For the next five years she and her husband were notable members of society in their hometown.

In 1999 Rania's life took a remarkable turn. On his deathbed King Hussein of Jordan changed the traditional line of succession. Instead of naming his brother as his successor, he chose his son, the crown prince of Jordan. Thus, Rania's husband, Abdullah, became the king of Jordan and she became the queen of a very influential Middle Eastern country.

Today Queen Rania travels the globe representing her country. Her three small children travel with her on most occasions and she is dedicated to helping the people of Jordan improve their lives. "Being queen is a responsibility," she has said. "It's not about putting on a costume."[4] She likens her position to running a very big and very serious business. "If my life had not gone in the direction it did, I would have pursued a career in the business world, but I would still have wanted to contribute to society."[5]

Queen Rania is deeply concerned with women's and children's rights. She works hard to promote international microfinance. Her mission is to help small business owners, many of them women, get financial backing for food stalls, beauty shops, carpet weaving businesses, and other enterprises. She wants to help lift families out of poverty. Microfinance respects people by saying they are good enough to receive a loan and will be trusted—and are expected—to pay it back while improving their business. It is more empowering than charity. She also works hard to prevent child abuse and honor killings, which are prevalent in Arab countries.

All the while she is still a mother and a wife. The king and queen of Jordan still live in the same house they lived in before they ruled their country. "I'm like any other professional woman; the biggest challenge is to do both things at the same time," says Queen Rania.[6] When the king came to meet her recently, just outside of Washington, D.C., Queen Rania waited patiently on the tarmac at an Air Force base for her husband to exit the plane. As he continued down the diplomatic reception line she eagerly watched the door. Finally, a small bespectacled boy and a tiny girl toting a Barbie book bag emerged. They ran down the stairs into Rania's waiting arms.

The queen then continued down the reception line with her daughter on her hip and her son in tow.[7]

There are other times when a circumstance in life seems to set you up for a mission. For example, three years after Marion Bunch's son died of AIDS, she saw an article in her Rotary Club bulletin. She says, "I heard a voice inside my ear saying, 'Come on, get up off your duff! It's time to do something.' So I started an AIDS education program in local schools."[8] Marion embraced the mission that seemed to have been thrust upon her by life.

When you are faced with a predetermined mission, you have a simple choice: accept it and embrace it wholeheartedly, or reject it. Don't try to accept it halfway. You'll be miserable, and the mission won't ever truly be your own. It is only when you fully embrace or own a mission that you can leave your own indelible mark on it, and infuse it with your creativity, your insight, and your unique talents and abilities.

Many singers choose to sing songs written by other people…but as they pour their own uniqueness into the rendition of that song, it becomes "their song," a hallmark of who they are as performers or artists. Choose to do the same with a mission that may have been written by someone else. Make it your own, and in the eyes of the world, the mission will be *yours*.

Set Your Mission "Big Enough"

Julie Burney is a retired police officer from Racine, Wisconsin. She started Cops 'N Kids Reading Center, Inc., to give kids a chance to get free books and learn to read. She has also organized police officers to hand out books to children while they patrol. She says her motivation is to "make [the kids] better students and better adults. I don't ever want to see a child without books."[9]

Kathryn Oliver is a marketing director for Price Waterhouse Coopers in Hartford, Connecticut. She says, "I volunteer at My Sisters' Place which is a local shelter for homeless women and their children. I truly believe in the strength of women coming together to help each other out."[10]

I don't know what your mission is or will be, but I do know this: you need to take all limits off your mission. Dream big and plan big.

The story is told of a man who came into the kitchen one day just in time to see his wife slice off the end of a roast before she put the roast into the roasting pan and then, into the oven. He asked her, "Honey, why did you cut off the end of the roast?" She said, "I don't know. I've just always done it."

"Well, why?" he insisted. She said, "I don't know…but Mom did it this way so I do it this way." He again asked, "Why?" She paused and said, "I don't know. I'll call and find out."

The woman's mother heard the question, laughed a bit, and then said, "That's a good question. I do it because Grandma did it that way. I don't know why. Call Grandma."

The woman called her grandmother and asked, "Grandma, why do we cut the end off the roast before we put it in the pan and then into the oven?" The grandmother said, "I cut off the end of the roast because my pan was too small for the whole roast!"

You may have been told all your life that there are some things you can't do…won't do…couldn't possibly do…or shouldn't try to do. Stop accepting those limitations. If a dream is burning in your heart, go for it. The person who tried to put a cap on your potential was very likely *wrong*.

Setting Goals with Heart and Soul

Your mission should encompass the desires of your heart, and your deepest hopes and wants. It does NOT need to be bound to your current profession or job. Sometimes what we truly want in life isn't what we are doing. Countless executives have found themselves in their fifties and sixties saying, "Is this all there is?" I recently heard about a man who counsels top executives as they retire from their corporate lives. He says that in eighty percent of the cases, the executive is looking for a significant change, saying, "My executive position didn't really make me feel fulfilled or satisfied." Many of the executives with whom he works take on something of a second career, pursuing the dream they always held secretly in their hearts—a dream they were afraid to pursue because they didn't think they'd make enough money or didn't think they could make it to the top.

Don't settle for a life that you one day reflect upon with an "I wish I had…" wistful longing. Pursue that dream now. None of us knows how long we will live. We can only live fully each day. Your mission statement should be one that, if you only live it FULLY for a day, will make you feel as if you have experienced purpose and meaning!

Through the years, I have met countless women who were getting paid to do one job but who had a passion for something else. That passion should be the place where you set goals and map out a mission. Take a look at the LONG VIEW of your life. See ways in which you can make a difference. In making a difference in the lives of others, you will find significance in your own life.

Your mission should be the most important thing in your mind and heart. You should hunger for it as if you hadn't eaten in days. It should make all other desires pale in comparison.

Write Out Your Mission Statement

Once you have reflected on who you are, what you want, how your dreams fit into the various roles you play daily…sit down and write out your mission statement. It should be no longer than a short paragraph, perhaps one to three sentences.

Live with that statement for a few days. If you don't feel excited and passionate about it, rewrite it!

Once the mission is set before you, go after it with all your heart and soul.

Keep It Alive. Here are some practical ways to keep your mission statement alive in your life:

- Carry your mission statement with you everywhere. In other words, put it in your day planner or your wallet. Pull it out periodically, perhaps as you ride a train into the city or wait for your next appointment. Commit it to memory so you can recall it readily.

- Record a message to yourself and include in that message your mission statement. Play this "memo to self" in your car.

- Talk to others about your mission and goals. Share your desire to live a truly successful life and ask people you trust to hold you accountable for accomplishing your mission. Ask them to check up on you and encourage you when you are struggling.

Practice Session

1. What is your purpose or mission in life? (Can you state it in fifty words or less?)

2. If you do not have a mission statement for your life…
   · What are your unique gifts, abilities, and skills?

   · What is your innermost desire? (What would you really be happy to achieve?)

   · Is there an issue or condition that really makes you "pound the table" because you get so upset about it?

   · What would cause you to weep if you left it "undone" during your life?

   · What sorts of activities give you the greatest sense of satisfaction?

3. Answer these questions:
   - What alterations do I want to make in myself? How does my mission statement challenge me to bring about these changes?

   - What alterations do I want to see in my family? How does my mission statement challenge me to bring about these changes?

   - What alterations do I want to see in my business? How does my mission statement challenge me to bring about these changes?

4. Read *The Purpose-Driven Life* by Rick Warren (Grand Rapids, MI: Zondervan, 2002). This book has helped me personally in ways too numerous for me to count.

- What alterations do I want to see in my friendships? How does my mission statement challenge me to bring about these changes?

- What alterations do I want to see in my neighborhood or community? How does my mission statement challenge me to bring about these changes?

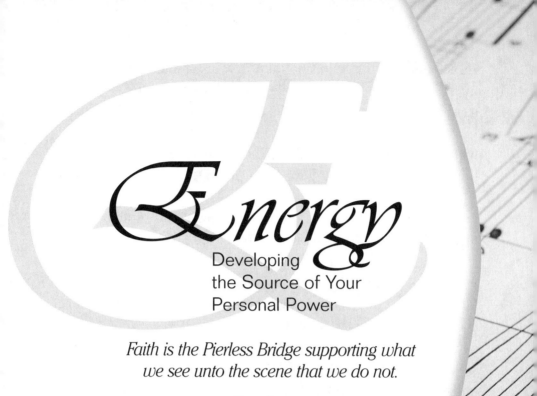

Energy

Developing
the Source of Your
Personal Power

*Faith is the Pierless Bridge supporting what
we see unto the scene that we do not.*

—Emily Dickinson

As a nurse and nun in Central Africa, Sister Maria experienced many difficulties in the hospital where she worked. One of the most difficult situations she faced happened one night in the labor ward. A mother who was about to deliver a baby came in with her two-year-old daughter. The midwives struggled to save this woman's life as she gave birth prematurely, but she did not survive.

The baby was also in serious trouble. Since the hospital had no electricity and there was no incubator for this newborn "preemie," a student midwife went in search of a box and some cotton wool in which to wrap the baby. Another student went to stoke the fire and fill a hot water bottle. The bottle burst as she was filling it. In tears, she reported this to Sister Maria.

Sister Maria quickly improvised. She instructed one of the women to sleep with the baby, lying as close to the fire as was safe and to keep it warm and free from drafts. The next morning the baby was still alive but did not have a steady heartbeat.

That day Sister Maria went to noon prayers with some of the children from the orphanage. She gave them suggestions of things to pray for, including the new baby and its two-year-old sister. During the prayer time a ten-year-old girl named Ruth prayed, "Please, God, send us a water bottle. It'll be no good tomorrow, God, as the baby will be dead, so please send it this afternoon. And while You are about it, please send a dolly for the little girl so she'll know You really love her."

Sister Maria felt put on the spot by this child's bold prayer. How could she honestly say, "Amen"? She wasn't sure God would answer Ruth's prayer and she knew that for the prayer to be answered, she would need to receive a package from someone back home. Even then, why would someone send a hot water bottle to the equator? Most people thought it was always hot in that part of Africa. In her four years of missionary service in Africa, nobody had ever sent such a thing to her. She felt it was ridiculous to even begin to expect such a miracle.

That afternoon as Sister Maria was teaching in the nurse's training school, a message was brought to her saying a car was waiting outside her home. By the time she arrived the car was gone, but on the front porch was a twenty-two-pound box. Surrounded by orphan children, Sister Maria opened the box and began to remove each item with care. There were hand-knitted sweaters for the children, bandages for the leprosy patients, and dried fruit for making cakes. Then Sister Maria reached into the box and pulled out a hot water bottle! As soon as Ruth saw the *hot water bottle*, she rushed forward crying, "If God sent the bottle, He must have sent the dolly, too!" She reached in to the bottom of the box…and pulled out a beautifully dressed doll!

That particular box had been in transit for more than five months by the time it reached Sister Maria. Parishioners from Sister Maria's home church had sent it. One member had heard God specifically instruct her to put a hot water bottle into the box; another had felt called to include a doll. They had no way of knowing their box would arrive on precisely the day those items were needed.

That day, in the heart of Africa, a baby was saved and a little girl was comforted because a group of women listened to the voices of their own hearts.

Are *you* listening to your heart today?

Are you consistently energizing your inner spirit, so that your spiritual heart has a message to speak?

Energizing your soul to meet life-altering challenges is the core component of your ability to find the stamina to accept, endure, or resist the challenges that come your way. Your ability to energize your soul is directly related to your ability to maintain moral standards, hold steadfast in the pursuit of your goals, and live out your relationships according to your deepest values.

Maintain Your Personal Core

At the core of your being are the values and beliefs that are "essentials." These are the beliefs that are rock-bottom for you. These are the values that you cannot violate and that you refuse to let others violate; they are the "line in the sand" that you do not cross.

At times, you need to post a "do not trespass" sign at the edge of your personal core to keep others from influencing, pushing, coddling, or taking advantage of you in ways that might entice you to abandon your values and beliefs. As long as you maintain a healthy core, you will have strength and energy to contribute to the world around you. If you allow this personal core to become compromised, you will be more likely to experience fear, shame, and regret. You also will likely lose a great deal of your inner confidence, power, and purpose.

Cultivate Your Spirituality

Angelique Du Toit is the founder of "Women, Arise!" She works with women to create balance in their lives. She has said, "In my experience of working with women, I have found that most of them live their lives looking forever outside themselves for solutions. Joy and balance can only come from within and you have to take responsibility for creating it."[1] I couldn't agree more.

It is out of your own spirituality that you are going to find solutions not only to the problems life throws at you, but to the problems you create for yourself!

In order to develop your spirituality, you need to have some "down time." This isn't just time to relax physically, but time to refresh yourself emotionally. It is time to meditate and turn your thoughts and feelings toward issues that are eternal, universal, and all-encompassing of life.

Ask yourself:

- Am I neglecting my spirituality?
- Am I setting time aside each day to nourish my spiritual self?
- Have I truly thought through and drawn some conclusions about what I consider to be the most important spiritual issues of life and death?

I personally have found it very beneficial to schedule twenty to thirty minutes a day for a "spiritual reflection time." This is a time for prayer, reading Scripture and other uplifting spiritual materials, and being quiet so I might reflect on what I have prayed and read.

Keep a Personal Journal. I also keep a personal journal. This is a way for me to be creative, private, and intensely personal about spiritual matters. I write something in my journal every day. Most of the entries are short. From time to time, I find it very helpful to read back through my journal to see various "trends" in my thinking and believing, as well as spiritual changes and growth. A journal is a great place to get critical thoughts out of your soul and onto paper—it's a very healthy form of release. The mind seems to be able to let go of some hurtful memories and negative attitudes once those instances and feelings are recorded on paper.

I also recommend that you use your journal to jot down funny incidents, write down a goal, and comment on the beauty around you. Record your feelings and your interactions with others. It doesn't really matter what you write as long as you write something that matters to you.

Listen to Your Heart. Part of becoming more alive spiritually means to be quiet and listen to life around you, as well as to the inner voice deep within. Anne Morrow Lindbergh wrote a beautiful passage about this in her book, *A Gift from the Sea*, which actually began as a personal daily journal. She wrote:

> At first the tired body takes over completely. As on shipboard, one descends into deck-chair apathy. One is forced against one's mind, against all tidy resolutions, back into the primeval rhythms of the seashore. Rollers on the beach, wind in the pines, the slow flapping of herons across sand dunes, drown out the hectic rhythms of city and suburb, time tables

and schedules. One should lie empty, open, without choice as a beach, waiting for a gift from the sea.[2]

Facing yourself alone, without distractions or others' opinions, can be difficult at first. If you've never done this, just being alone with yourself can be daunting. It is also highly motivating.

Some people find gardening, drawing, sketching, painting, doing needlework, or taking long leisurely walks to be good methods for getting in touch with their own inner core. The point is to spend some time thinking about self and the biggest issues of life:

- Who am I?
- Am I happy?
- Why am I here?
- What happens after life?
- Am I living up to my potential—or am I in active pursuit of it?
- What should happen next in my life?
- How should I change or grow?

Learn to Be Alone

My daughter has a friend who spends one week each year in Arizona at a Roman Catholic convent where she doesn't speak the entire time. She also says that spending time with the nuns in the abbey, in silence, allows her to focus on her spirituality and personal development. She says that the energy she gets from that one week can carry her through an entire year of job stress, family strife, and personal growing pains.

Now, this may not seem like *your* cup of tea, but if it's not, take time to find out what your cup of tea might be! Find something that suits your personality and plan it into your schedule. You will benefit greatly from the boost that a personal spiritual retreat can give you.

I have met numerous women through the years who have never been alone. From the time they were teenagers they always had boyfriends, and then maybe got married young or right out of college. As adults they have never been alone. If this describes you, then you are a blessed individual. But you are probably also an individual who functions or has functioned in the shadow of another person. You may have lived a life that revolved around children. You may never have taken the time to develop yourself as an individual woman with special talents, desires, and goals.

Now is the time to do so.

Other women may be in a position of suddenly finding they have lost a spouse, or that they have an "empty nest" with all of their children off to college or careers. Such women often feel adrift. By necessity, they also have to learn to be alone and to develop *themselves*. They, too, need to discover their talents, desires, and goals.

Whatever your situation in life may be, NOW is a good time to learn HOW to be alone with yourself…and like it.

Learning to be alone may very well be the scariest thing you have ever attempted. This is especially true if you've always relied on other people to make key decisions or choices for you. So…face up to that fear. Embrace the challenge as an opportunity to discover more about who you are and what you can do. Take the opportunity to uncover your hidden talents, reveal your secret dreams, and expose the real you.

Spending quality time *alone* is essential to fostering your spirituality and energizing your life.

Cultivate Your Emotional Life

Women are distinctly different from men in their emotional lives. I realize that is a blanket summary, but I do believe it is a statement that applies to the vast cross-section of the female population. Women need far more "relational" time than men do. Two men might be energized by playing golf, watching a sporting event, or working on a car, never exchanging more than a dozen statements during the entire time they are together. Not so with women! Women can feel energized by having a good conversation while they are folding clothes or stuffing envelopes.

There are a number of ways to rejuvenate your emotional life. Just about any activity that allows you to feel "better" about yourself after you complete the activity counts! Consider how you are likely to feel if you do the following:

- Organize a monthly luncheon with a group of women who have similar goals and values. Use this time to encourage one another in your quest to meet your goals and live out your values.

- Set aside a weekend to throw away items that are cluttering up your home, such as old newspapers, magazines, coupons, and junk mail. Organize your pantry. Create files that have all your emergency information, a household maintenance schedule, or appliance warranties. I like what William Morris has said on this subject: "Have nothing in your houses that you do not know to be useful or believe to be beautiful."

- Learn a new skill, even if it is how to play poker, use chopsticks, or install a program on your computer.

- Clear out your clothes closet, creating a pile of items to give to a charity in your community.

- Volunteer your time at a women's shelter, soup kitchen, classroom, or community center.

Each of the four activities in the last item listed above is more fun and also more emotionally rewarding to a woman if she does them with a friend!

Sometimes it is emotionally enriching for a woman just to read...to contemplate...to stare at a beautiful vista with her feet propped up...or to take a stroll through a park. Do what causes you to say at the end of the activity, "That felt great. I feel refreshed and renewed."

The more you cultivate your emotional life...cultivate your spiritual life...and reflect upon who you ARE as a unique, valuable, and lovable person...the stronger your inner core will become. And the stronger your inner core, the greater your personal power and confidence will grow.

Practice Session

1. Do you sometimes feel as if you are projecting a "self" that is not the real inner you? Do you sometimes project on the outside that you have it all together, even when things are crumbling on the inside? Describe how you feel when you do this.

2. Name three things that you can do THIS WEEK to enrich your spiritual life.

   1) _____

   2) _____

   3) _____

3. Name three things you can do THIS WEEK to enrich your emotional life.

   1) _____

   2) _____

   3) _____

4. In fifty words or less, reflect on how your BUSINESS life is made better by the fact that you have a strong spiritual and emotional center. (How does your business tend to suffer if you are not strong spiritually?)

5. In fifty words or less, reflect on how your FAMILY life is made better by the fact that you have a strong spiritual and emotional center. (How does your family life suffer if you are not strong spiritually?)

6. Identify several things that tend to assault your personal circle of core beliefs and character.

What can you do to reinforce your spiritual core so it can repel these negative forces?

focus

The Challenge of "Holding the Note"

Change is not made without inconvenience.

—Richard Hooker
(Quoted in the preface of Samuel Johnson's
Dictionary of the English Language,
published in 1755)

CHAPTER

7

A couple was watching television when the woman said, "I'm tired, and it's getting late. I think I'll go to bed." She went to the kitchen to make sandwiches for the next day's lunches, rinsed out the popcorn bowls, took meat out of the freezer for supper the following evening, checked the cereal box levels, filled the sugar container, put spoons and bowls on the table, and prepared the coffeepot so it would be ready to go first thing in the morning. Then she put some wet clothes in the dryer, put a load of clothes into the washing machine, ironed a shirt and secured a loose button, picked up the game pieces left on the table, put the telephone book back into its drawer, watered the plants in the dining room, emptied a wastebasket, hung up a towel to dry, then yawned, stretched, and headed for the bedroom. On the way she stopped by her desk and wrote a note to her child's teacher, and counted out some cash for the next day's field trip. She pulled a textbook out from its hiding place under a chair, signed a birthday card for a friend and addressed and stamped the envelope, scribbled a quick grocery list, and put both the card and list in her purse.

Making it to the bathroom, she washed her face and put on moisturizer, brushed and flossed her teeth, and trimmed her nails. Her husband called out, "I thought you were going to bed." She replied, "I'm on my way!" But first, she put some water in the dog's dish and put the cat outside, made sure the doors were locked, looked in on two of their children, turned out a bedside lamp, hung up a shirt, and threw some dirty socks in the hamper. She had a brief conversation with her teenager who was still up doing homework. In her own room, she set the alarm, laid out clothing for the next day, straightened up the shoe rack a bit, and added three things to her list of things to do the next day. About that time, her husband turned off the television set and announced to no one in particular, "I'm going to bed." He got up and went straight to bed without giving anything else a second thought.

Can you relate? Both those who are married and those who are single seem to be finding that life is in constant motion from the time they get up in the morning to the time they go to bed. Everything seems to take longer than expected and to be in constant motion.

In music, we who are singers face the challenge at times of "holding a note" for sustained beats, sometimes several measures. A singer at times feels as if he or she is being asked to exhale longer than it was possible to inhale. The sustained note, however, is often the difference between a piece of music being perceived as fluid and transitional, or choppy and segmented—which in turn can mean the difference between a melodic line being beautifully expressed or lost to the listener's ear. As is true in life, fluid, transitional, and melodic in the music realm are better than choppy, segmented, and lost!

Overcoming Intrusions and Storms

Any number of things can come against you to try to throw you off course. Crises occur, tragedies happen, people get sick, and sometimes people we love die. These strong currents of pain, sorrow, and disruption can threaten to capsize us. Don't allow it to happen.

Certainly you must take the time for healthy grieving and recovery…but then, get back on track toward your potential. Don't allow a difficult time to become a permanent difficulty. Recognize that all problems have a lifespan, and that if you will only choose to endure to the end of a problem—learning what you can and receiving the help and comfort of others willing to be supportive of you—you can emerge from a problem situation stronger, wiser, and more motivated than ever before.

In times of crisis or extreme difficulty, choose to continue your spiritual disciplines. Continue to nourish your body, mind, and spirit with good "food"—good foods in the natural, but also good, encouraging, and uplifting ideas and materials that will keep your soul refreshed and alive. Continue to guard yourself against negative people, negative values, and your own negative thoughts and feelings. Don't be sucked into other people's quagmire of negativity. Do what it takes to refresh, renew, and rejuvenate your life.

At the Winter Olympics in Salt Lake City I spent an evening with my children watching the short speed-skating competition. I was amazed to see men and women race at breakneck speeds. I soon realized that it wasn't how fast they skated that ensured a win—it was how *smart* they raced. Each racer had a strategy for making the most of each lap, knowing when to come up with a burst of energy to pass a competitor and when to hold back and lean into a turn. Adopt that perspective. At times when you feel yourself becoming exhausted, hold back a bit. Renew your energy. Think "smarter."

Three Keys to Developing Focus

If you don't have a sharp enough focus to your life, I encourage you to consider doing the following:

1. **Make the Most of a Mentor.** A personal mentor can help you focus your life in any number of ways. Mentors come in many styles:

   - *A Personal Mentor.* This person is a counselor or friend who knows you well and cares about your development and success so much that he or she will tell you the truth about your strengths and weaknesses. A personal mentor should understand how you operate, how you respond to criticism, and how well you take compliments. He or she should genuinely want to see you succeed and be willing to invest time and energy in meetings with you to encourage you, advise you, listen to you, and counsel you on things to consider as you pursue your goals.

   - *A Spiritual Counselor.* This is a person of wisdom who understands the universal truths of life and will help you grapple with issues related to your faith and to your character and integrity.

- *A Specialist in Your Area of Concern.* If you are having family problems, you need to find a family counselor or specialist. If you are dealing with management or strategic planning problems, you need to seek out a pro in the area of management or strategic planning.

- *A Practical Counselor.* This is a friend who has had lots of life experience and who is highly concerned about what works and doesn't work. This person is one who will give you very practical tips on what to do or not to do to reach a specific goal.

At times you may find that a person fills more than one of these roles. At times you may find that you get these four types of wisdom from a small group of friends with whom you meet on a regular basis. These friends may be from your place of worship or your neighborhood, or professionals from your workplace or your general career area.

Those who help you focus your life need to be open, honest, and character- driven. You should *admire* the people from whom you receive counsel. You should be able to look at their lives and say, "I want to be more like her" or "I want to reflect his character." Look for people who have a track record of success in their lives, and who can keep a confidence.

2. **Work on Your Ability to Concentrate.** A vital dimension of focusing relates to your own ability to concentrate. People can give you wise counsel, but if you do not discipline your own mind to learn from them and apply what they counsel you to do, you will be wasting your time and theirs. Be attentive to what others say to you, and then immediately seek ways to apply their wisdom to your life. Write down the key points they make. Commit key concepts to memory and quote them to yourself frequently. If a mentor recommends a particular book to you, buy it and read it. Underline key passages and make notes. Pursue your goals with single-minded FOCUS.

Knowledge is increasing at such a rate that even those with advanced degrees in any discipline find that MOST of what they studied is obsolete in six to eight years. In the high-tech areas, knowledge tends to be replaced every two to three years. You must keep learning!

As you read and study, ask yourself questions such as these:

- What is the real issue here?
- What does this mean, and, in particular, what does this mean in a practical way to my life, my family, my business?
- How does this relate to other articles or books I have read?
- Are there flaws in this logic or in this idea?
- How does this information fit in with what I believe to be universal and absolute principles?

And then ask yourself very practical questions, especially if what you are reading or studying relates to character issues:

- How do I begin to practice this truth?
- What do I need to change?
- How can I make this principle come about in my life, beginning today?

Change is important. Learning is vital. To the best of your ability, make sure you are learning the BEST principles and truths, and that you are getting the most current and reliable information. And then, make sure you are applying this information and these truths to your life in ways that are in line with your core beliefs and goals. Continue to grow.

3. **Choose to Learn from Mistakes.** Errors happen. There's no way around them. Nobody is perfect and not only are we prone to making mistakes, but we live, work, and are in association with people who make mistakes. You can learn good and valuable lessons from these oftentimes-painful experiences, including the mistakes that you yourself were guilty of making.

Don't get bogged down in that failure or mistake. Don't allow the situation to take on monumental proportions. Immediately ask yourself:

- What might I learn from this mistake?
- What can I do to ensure that I don't make this mistake again?
- What good things might come from this?
- How can I get past this and move on to more productive and positive activities and experiences?

Maintain a joyful attitude *in spite of the problem* you may be experiencing. No problem has a built-in power to destroy a cheerful or optimistic attitude unless YOU allow that problem to have such power. Choose to remain optimistic even in the face of difficulty. In so doing, you will draw people to you, both to comfort you and help you. Pessimism and negativity repel people, and in times of trouble or difficulty, the last thing you need is to push people away who may be able to help you solve your problem.

The art of the mid-course correction is an art worth mastering.

Learn the Art of "Creative Adjustment"

Music is filled with themes…and variations on themes. The one thing to note about a variation on a theme is that it still conveys the theme! There may have been a creative adjustment of some kind, but the basic melody continues to shine through. The same holds true for your pursuit of life goals. Creative adjustments may need to be made along the way, but always with an eye toward your pursuit of the goals and priorities that are of utmost importance to you.

Margaret Rudkin was an early pioneer in business. She had a successful career on Wall Street in the early 1920s. Then she quit that career when she married and moved with her husband to a horse farm in Connecticut. She liked living off her farm and feeding her family wholesome foods, but she couldn't find bread that she felt was healthy. All of the bread products in the stores were made from highly processed flour. So Margaret began to play with an old bread recipe given to her by her grandmother. She fiddled with the ingredients and baking process until she found just the right mix of whole-grain ingredients for the texture and taste she liked. Then she asked a local mill to grind unprocessed flour for her. She began to bake her bread and market it locally. She was bold enough to ask for twenty-five cents a loaf when all other bread was ten cents a loaf. But, the quality of her product was unmistakable and within five years she was selling two million loaves a year!

Was Margaret creative? Certainly! She looked at a staple of life in a new way. Did she adapt? Yes. She didn't like what she saw and she came up with a game plan for change. And...she continued to adapt.

Other bread companies began to copy Margaret's recipe and to sell healthy bread products, so Margaret felt the need to make an adjustment in her business plan. She went to Europe to see what was happening there. She developed a real love for European cookies and she partnered with a Belgian baker to create a line of cookies that she named after famous European cities—for example, the Milano cookie.

Yes, Margaret Rudkin was the mother of Pepperidge Farms. She catered to customers with discriminating tastes in an ordinary market. She eventually sold her company to Campbell's Foods in 1960 when her stock was worth twenty-eight million dollars. Not bad for a mom on a farm in Connecticut.[1]

Do what *you* need to do to creatively adjust your life. Stay true to your inner values. Stay focused on your goals...yet be flexible in your methods. There is a RIGHT way for *you* to get from point A to point B. Find it!

Crisis and Creative Adjustments

Many times, a crisis or emergency situation either forces or presents a unique opportunity for a person to make a creative adjustment. Many a person has moved, changed careers, or gone back to school in the wake of a flood, hurricane, serious health issue, major corporate layoff, or other time of tumult and turmoil.

I have a friend named Iris who lives in Brazil. Like many women today, Iris's life was filled with countless activities that go along with being a wife and mother. Then, her husband left her for another woman. Iris's husband was the only man Iris had ever loved, and when he abandoned her, she felt a great blow to her self-confidence. She suddenly found herself alone and responsible for caring for herself and her son. She felt depressed, but she kept moving forward instead of letting circumstances control the outcome of her life.

Some time prior to her marriage, Iris had started and had nearly completed coursework for a doctorate. Six months after her husband left her, she decided to continue her pursuit of that goal.

Iris faced a great deal of paperwork in filing for an extension on her studies. She left some of that paperwork for a secretary to type one evening. Several nights later a woman called Iris at home. She said:

> I read your paperwork requesting an extension to complete your degree. I don't know you but I know your story. I, too, was left by the only man I ever loved while I was pregnant with our second child. That was eight years ago and I thought I would never recover. But I soon had two wonderful children to care for, so with the help of my friends I started to study again and received a degree.
>
> Last year I was promoted two times and now it is my turn to help someone who needs an opportunity. I just want you to know that I will personally take your paperwork to the committee. I will walk it through for you and deal with any problems or questions that may arise. My only request of you is

that you begin now to study for your degree. When the committee makes their decision about whether to grant you an extension or not, you must be prepared. The more work you have completed, the better your chances will be.

The committee gave Iris six weeks to complete her degree. With the support of friends and family members Iris worked full-time on her dissertation. Her friends helped her to meet expenses, bought her food, and cared for her son. One week before the deadline Iris's research partner became so ill that he had to be hospitalized. His wife was away at medical school so another friend of Iris's took care of him while Iris completed the final chapters of her dissertation. The dissertation was turned in and the necessary copies were made and left for her committee *one minute before the deadline!* Two months later Iris defended her dissertation in front of her committee. She now holds a doctor of philosophy degree in Portuguese Philology and Language.

Iris had determination. With a very clear-cut choice to make, she chose to take a great risk in her life and not let circumstances keep her from reaching a good goal. She was willing to rely on the kindness of others to help her through this difficult struggle, but she was the one who took the risk and achieved success.

What about you?

What do you need to do today to reach a goal?

Do you need to make a creative adjustment?

Are you letting a negative situation determine the outcome of your life? It's time to adjust your life creatively and maintain FOCUS.

Creatively Adjust Your Thinking

There are times in your life when a creative adjustment is not a matter of a career choice or of getting back on track with a business goal. Rather, the necessary adjustment involves the way you think.

The creative adjustment may mean learning to face up to and deal with those negative things that *can* be remedied in your life, and then letting other negative words, situations, and attitudes roll on by. A creative adjustment always means that you do whatever it takes to maintain your FOCUS on the good things in life, to be thankful, and to choose to be positive.

There is a huge difference between escapism and allowing negatives in your life to roll on by. Escapism, like denial, is a form of ignoring or running away from negative situations. For a number of years I tried "escapism" as a way of dealing with problems. I knew things were not going well in my marriage, but instead of seeking counsel, I buried myself in work and travel. I often worked twelve-to-fifteen-hour days. That kind of schedule doesn't fit well with being a wife and mother. But, I got good at rationalizing my actions by telling myself how much my family needed the money. In many ways I was running from my life instead of building my life.

To live a genuinely successful life—one with peace of mind and harmony from the inside out—you must face up to your problems, and deal with them, spurred on by optimism and hope for the future.

We all know people who seem to wallow in the negative. We call them killjoys, negative Nellies, and pessimists. They always seem to have a sarcastic comment, criticism, or jibe. They insist on playing devil's advocate although you've never heard them play any other role. They bring people down and often create discord wherever they go.

Negativism can be a major roadblock on your path to success. First, it takes a tremendous amount of energy to maintain a negative attitude all the time. Just think what could be accomplished if that energy could be turned to creating solutions!

Certainly there are plenty of things in our world today about which a person can be negative. Some people find the fast-paced life of these times to be a burden—they struggle with changes in technology and a seemingly endless parade of opportunities that require them to make choices and adjustments.

Other people see negativism as a form of emotional protection. They may have been deeply hurt or their self-esteem may have taken a serious hit, and they resort to cynicism, sarcasm, and pessimism to cover their scars. The truth, however, is that negativism rarely fools anybody. It is an outward sign of inward misery.

The music world is filled with talented and beautiful people. None is as amazing to me, however, as a young man named Thomas Quastoff from Germany. He has a bass voice that can move even thick-skinned people to tears. As he sings the works of the masters such as Bach, Schubert, and Mendelssohn, you get the sense that he was truly blessed by God with his vocal ability. But what makes Thomas extra special are the circumstances of his life.

If you just *heard* Thomas and didn't *see* Thomas, you might assume that his hauntingly beautiful voice comes from a tall, dark, and handsome body. In actuality, Thomas is four feet tall. He has fingers protruding from his shoulders and he has no knees. He was a Thalidomide baby and when he was born, most people thought his physical deformities also meant mental limitations. His first memories are of waking up in a psychiatric hospital and hearing people screaming.

Eventually someone in the mental hospital discovered that Thomas was not mentally challenged in any way; in fact, he was very gifted intellectually and also musically.

Thomas often tells the story of being in Vienna for a concert. He was staying in a particular hotel that he liked, in part because the staff was so helpful to him with his physical challenges. One of the helpful things they did was to put a stool in the elevator so he could reach to push the buttons. One night he came back, entered the elevator, and once the doors were shut, he realized the stool had been removed. He was stuck. He couldn't reach the buttons...so he started singing. He said he had to sing for a long time—and very loudly—before someone realized he was stuck.

Thomas doesn't tell stories like these with bitterness in his voice. Instead, he laughs. He understands that his life is different in some ways from others around him, but he has made a choice to be positive and to share his wonderful gift in generous ways with the world. He has learned to replace negatives with positives.

Thomas and I became good friends on a singing tour in Japan. We were touring with Gachinger Kantorei from Stuttgart, Germany, with Helmuth Rilling conducting. I was in the chorus and Thomas was the baritone soloist. As we hurried through airports on a rather frantic travel schedule, Thomas would sometimes hop on the front of a luggage cart and allow someone to push him through the terminal so he could keep up with the group. There he would sit, smiling and sometimes singing as he moved through the crowds.

One day Thomas asked me, "Beverly, have you had much sadness in your life?"

"Oh, yes," I responded.

He said, "That explains why you are always so happy. I have had sadness, too. I choose to be happy."

How is it that you face the difficulties and negative situations of your life? Do you *choose* to be happy?

Pessimists invariably ask, "Why me? Why now? Why this?"

Optimists are those who ask, "What can I do? How can I learn from this? How can I grow from this? How can I change this situation?"

Pessimists look at what is, in the light of what was. If they look to the future at all, they look at what might go wrong. The pessimist makes statements such as, "I'm not very smart," "I can't do anything right," or "I'm never going to get well."

Optimists look at what *can* be. The optimist makes statements such as, "I'm learning something new," "I can get this right," and "I'll soon be back on my feet."

Optimism and a quest for one's potential go hand-in-glove.

This seems especially true in the workplace. Pessimists see their jobs as being dead ends. They always find something to complain about. Their negative comments tend to bring down morale, which in turn impacts productivity and quality.

In contrast, optimism compels people to higher morale, greater productivity, and increased quality.

"But I'm a critical thinker," some people say. A critical thinker is a person who faces a difficult situation and says, "What's the best way through this problem? What's the best solution? What's the best choice or decision?" There's nothing incompatible with being a critical thinker and an optimist. If a critical thinker is truly a pessimist, the result is likely to be no decisions, no solutions, and no way through a problem, because the difficulty will be perceived as being insurmountable or unbeatable.

Critical thinkers see outside the box. Pessimists see themselves in the box forever.

As a musician, I especially like Emily Dickinson's little poem:

> Hope is the thing with feathers
> That perches in the soul
> And sings the tunes without the words,
> And never stops at all.

Choose to sing a song of optimism in your soul!

What It Takes to Make a Creative Attitude Adjustment

Let me suggest four steps a person can take to make a creative attitude adjustment and move from pessimism to optimism.

1. **Make a Change Over Time.** Attitudes rarely change overnight. For most people, going from pessimism to optimism does not occur suddenly or easily. The process takes intention, time, and an ongoing accountability to yourself, and perhaps to someone who will help you change your outlook.

   I like to think in terms of the music words *crescendo* and *diminuendo*. A crescendo involves a gradual increase in volume, sometimes over several measures. A diminuendo involves a gradual decrease in volume. For most people, an infusion of positive attitudes and optimism involves the gradual increase of thinking, speaking, and acting positively...and at the same time, working toward a gradual decrease of those things that we might call worries, fears, negative thoughts, and pessimistic speech.

Seek a CRESCENDO in the amount of time you spend reading, seeing, hearing, and thinking about things that are positive. Work for a DIMINUENDO in the amount of time you spend reading, seeing, and thinking about things that are negative—including news reports or fictitious stories that include violence, terror, brutality, abuse, graphic sexual portrayals, swear words and "gutter" language, and other immoral behavior and speech.

2. **Focus on the Solution.** This doesn't mean we resign ourselves to living with problems forever, but rather, we simply acknowledge that problems exist. We recognize that life is hard, challenges spring up, and crises hit us, often when we feel least prepared to handle them. Yes, problems exist, but *so do solutions.*

Sometimes there's a fine line between accepting a problem and challenging a problem. My daughter Debi experienced this several years ago. She left a jacket at the security checkpoint in the Los Angeles International Airport. When she realized what she had done, she immediately called to find out if the jacket had been turned in to the Lost and Found department. It had been. The person in that department who answered the phone assured her the jacket would be kept until her return to Los Angeles several days later.

When Debi returned to L.A., she went to the Lost and Found desk and asked for her jacket. It took four people looking in three drawers to conclude that her jacket was nowhere to be found. Debi immediately began to suggest several places the jacket may have been put—perhaps in a back office, at another

Lost and Found station—or perhaps it was still at the security checkpoint where she had left it in the first place. She was met with a wall of pessimism.

Certainly this was a problem, but Debi wasn't about to assume it was an unsolvable problem!

Debi went home and began to make calls. It took several calls before a manager finally told her that her jacket, indeed, had been located in a back office. She suggested that the manager mail the jacket to her at her expense. Again, pessimism and negativity reared their heads. This wasn't "regular procedure" even though the manager admitted that sending a COD package would cost his department nothing. In all, what should have taken five to ten minutes of Debi's time after she returned to the airport took several hours over several days.

Now, Debi could have accepted this problem as a *perpetual* problem and given up all hope of ever seeing her jacket again. Or, she could have accepted that the problem existed, but that it was a *temporary and solvable* problem. She chose the latter.

The distinction is an important one to make. Some problems are long-term and may seem perpetual. Others are short-term, even momentary. Make the distinction, and then move on to identify and develop a *solution*.

3. **Make a GOOD Choice to Negate a BAD Choice.** A good choice can negate or overcome a bad choice.

    Many times we start out with the best of intentions and then, we make a poor choice or someone around us makes a poor choice and we fall off the track of success. The solution to a bad choice is to make a BETTER choice that overcomes the original bad choice. Don't be afraid to decide, to choose, to take a risk. Don't allow a problem to paralyze you so that you sink into indecision and do nothing about your problem. Take action. Make choices that have the potential to turn around a negative situation.

- Get wise counsel from others.

- Consider all your options.

- Look for the practical solution that will result in the best possible outcome for all who might be involved in the problem.

- Find ways to continue caring for others.

- Maintain a positive outlook and an attitude of hope.

- Double-check your *purpose* in life. Refocus on what you believe gives your life significance. Put your solution-oriented efforts into those activities that give your life the most meaning and bring you the greatest fulfillment.

- Finally, believe the best of other people. Surround yourself with people who treat you with respect and who value you. Treat them in like manner— respect others and value their ideas, help, input, feelings, and above all, their dignity.

When you believe the best of other people, you will be open to hearing their ideas and suggestions. Open yourself up to the idea that there's more than one way to solve most problems. Get out of the rut of your own thinking and make room for new perspectives on your problem. At the same time, don't just automatically accept another person's solution; make sure the solution that seems to be right to them also seems right to you.

4. Cast Off the Negative Circumstance. There comes a point where you may need to "cast off" a negative circumstance rather than wallow around in it any longer. Some problems loom so large, and for so long, that they threaten to destroy us or to forever keep us from the pursuit of our potential.

For example, the day may come when you realize that you truly do need to sell your home and fancy car and "downsize" your life a little in order to "cast off" the problem of monthly bills that never seem to be paid in full.

You may need to give up your personal struggle with alcohol and get into a rehab program and then into follow-up support groups.

You may need to walk away from the abusive relationship once and for all.

Rather than allow a problem to pull you deeper and deeper into perpetual depression, sickness, suffering, or sorrow, take charge of the problem and take responsibility for your own life. Chart a course to a brighter future. Break free! Believe for the best you can be and begin to live a life that reflects your belief. Begin to do the things that bring you purpose, meaning, and deep joy.

One of the greatest and bravest examples I know of a person who has turned negatives into positives in her life is my friend Stephanie Fast. She is the daughter of a Korean mother and an American soldier father. In Korea, Stephanie was looked down upon because of her mixed-race heritage. When Stephanie was three years old, her mother put her on a bus and told her that her uncle would pick her up in the next city. Stephanie got off the bus and waited for hours for her uncle to come get her. Finally a policeman came to her and told her she had no uncle.

Can you imagine the fear that must have filled this little girl's heart? She began to live on the streets at the age of three! She lived with a pack of other children and for six years, she survived by stealing food and sleeping under bridges and in abandoned buildings.

One night Stephanie was sleeping with another child in the basement of an old building. She awoke to find that her friend had died by her side and rats were beginning to chew at the body. She managed to crawl outside, only to fall unconscious from lack of food and sleep. A passerby thought she was dead and threw her into a garbage dump. A World Vision nurse found her there and took her to their hospital. She nursed Stephanie back to health and after many months of recovery and counseling, Stephanie was adopted by an American family and moved to the United States.

Today Stephanie speaks frequently about her past to various groups, but as she relates this terrible saga of her early years, she doesn't focus on the problems. Instead, she focuses on the love she received from her American family. She speaks about the power of love and the ways in which love heals and strengthens even the most broken life.[2]

I don't care what negatives you may have in your life, either past or present. Make the creative adjustment necessary and seek a way to give love out of your pain, sorrow, disappointment, or discouragement. In giving love, you will receive love. The love you receive back into your life may not come from the person to whom you are giving love. It may come from a completely different person or source. But it will come. Love is truly what enables us to eliminate negatives permanently, and to live continually on the positive side of life.

Carrot, Egg, or Coffee?

To a very great extent, the way in which you handle adversity in your life will determine your future success. If you allow adversity to teach you, shape you, and mold you into a more balanced life and a greater purpose, then adversity will have served you well. On the other hand, if you allow adversity to overwhelm you and dash your hopes and dreams, then you will be serving adversity. The choice is yours.

There's a wonderful story that illustrates this point.

A young woman went to her mother and told her about her many problems. The daughter just didn't know how she was going to make it through this difficult time—she felt like giving up on all fronts. The fight and struggles at work and home were draining all of her energy and depleting all her joy.

Her mother took her to the kitchen. She then proceeded to fill three pots with water. In the first she placed a bunch of carrots. In the second she placed several eggs. In the third she placed some ground coffee beans.

The mother set the pots on three burners of the stove and turned the heat on high so that the pots boiled. She continued to listen to her daughter's problems for the next twenty minutes and then she turned off the burners. She fished out the carrots and placed them in a bowl. Then she pulled the eggs from the boiling water and placed them in a bowl. Finally, she ladled the coffee into a couple of mugs. Turning to her daughter, the mother said, "Tell me what you see."

"Carrots, eggs, and coffee," the young woman replied.

The mother brought her closer and asked her to feel the carrots. She did, and noted that they were soft. The mother then asked her to take an egg and break it. After the daughter pulled off the shell, she observed that the egg was hard-boiled. Finally, the mother asked her to sip the coffee. The daughter smiled and commented on the rich aroma and flavor.

She then asked her mother, "So what's the point, Mom?"

Her mother said, "Each of these items faced the same adversity: boiling water. Each reacted differently. The carrots initially were hard and strong. The boiling water caused them to become soft and weak. The egg had been fragile. But after experiencing the boiling water, the insides of the egg became hard. The ground coffee beans responded in quite a different manner. After they were placed in the boiling water…they changed the water!

"Which are you going to be?" the mother then asked her daughter. "When adversity knocks on your door, how are you going to respond? Will you allow adversity to weaken you so that you have no strength, no courage, no inner confidence? Will you allow adversity to turn you into a bitter person with a hard heart? Or will you find a way to release all of the built-in fragrance and flavor of your life? Will you emerge from this troubled time better or worse?"

How about you?

Choose to Persevere

The dictionary defines perseverance as "holding to a course of action, belief or purpose without giving way." That takes courage and grit! In the end, ONLY those who persevere in holding their FOCUS reach their potential.

Some of the world's greatest inventions were developed by people who practiced tireless perseverance. They were people who refused to give up or become so discouraged that they turned away from a compelling creative idea. Ordinary items such as paper clips, Post-it™ notes, and even paper bags are all products of perseverance.

Margaret Knight was born in Maine in 1838. When she was twelve she worked in a mill where she saw a man get seriously injured by a machine on the factory floor. She thought about the accident night and day and finally, after trying and retrying her ideas, she came up with a stop-motion device that shut down the machine entirely when it malfunctioned. The mill immediately began to use her invention and many lives were saved through the years as a result.

At the age of thirty Margaret got a patent for a machine that could make the square bottoms of paper bags. As an employee of the Columbia Paper Bag Company she had spent countless hours working on a wooden machine that could cut, fold, and paste the bag bottoms. She went through thousands of bags. Her employer was upset about the amount of time she spent on her invention, but Margaret offered to sell him the rights to the machine once she had perfected it. He accepted her offer. Unfortunately, before Margaret could have an iron model of her machine made for the patent, a man who had seen her prototype beat her to the patent office.

Margaret put up a fight, filed a patent interference suit, and spent a hundred dollars a day plus expenses for sixteen days of depositions from herself and other key witnesses. The man claimed

that because Knight was a woman, she could not possibly understand the mechanical complexities of the machine. Margaret persevered. She had kept careful notes, diary entries, and samples. The court recognized her expertise and ruled in her favor. She then sold her machine to the Eastern Paper Bag Company for a significant fee, plus dividends and royalties.

During her lifetime Margaret Knight patented more than twenty inventions. She worked on rotary engines, motors for automobiles, and a successful shoe-cutting device. When Margaret saw a problem, she immediately began to think of a way to solve it…and she persevered until she did.[3]

FOCUS and Margaret's kind of perseverance are virtually synonymous.

Perseverance in Overcoming Discouragement and Difficulty

It's difficult to persevere if you feel your dreams have been dashed or you've lost your courage. Nevertheless…persevere!

Bernice Hansen is a person who has triumphed at staying focused and making creative adjustments throughout her life. In 1949 she and her husband went door to door selling vitamin supplements. Bernice had no sales experience and was scared to death, but she persevered because she had little money and three children to feed. Over the years she built a network of vitamin distributors and a successful company. She was widowed twice, but she continued to build her network, which today includes many other product items and is now online. She has distributors in her group from around the world and is known and loved by millions of people. Now in her nineties, she still has abundant energy and a joyful outlook on life. I have never heard her complain. I have always found her ready and willing to meet the challenges of an ever-changing world. She has taught me a great deal about how to make creative adjustments so that I might remain focused on my goals and my potential!

I believe perseverance is largely a matter of

- sailing in the right direction
- remaining steadfast and "on course"
- being determined to weather any storms and finish the task.

Always, always, always keep the big picture of your goal at the forefront of your thinking.

Abigail was a woman who did this. She lived in the late 1700s and when she married, she expected to live a quiet life in a rural setting while her husband practiced law. Then her husband, John, was elected to participate in something innovative called a "Continental Congress." He was away for months while she remained at home in Braintree, Massachusetts, tending the farm, raising her children, and writing volumes of letters to encourage and motivate her husband.

When the Revolutionary War broke out, Abigail was on the front lines. She lived not far from Boston Harbor and no doubt had a front-row seat for the British invasion and subsequent fighting. When her husband and son both traveled overseas to try to gain the support of France and Holland for America's cause, Abigail remained at home. Her letters kept her husband updated on the status of the fighting.

It would have been no surprise to anyone if Abigail had turned bitter or resentful at the amount of time her husband spent away from the family. But Abigail Adams was a woman of substance, bright intellect, and devoted patriotism. She saw the "bigger picture"—the birth of a great nation. And it was her constant vision for the future that kept her on course.[4]

Never, never, never lose sight of your goals. They are the horizon toward which you must sail each day. Never lose sight of your mission, your priorities, your most deeply held principles and beliefs. Keep them in the forefront of your thinking. They will help you persevere.

Keep your focus on the guideposts that line the path to your future. The more clearly you define your potential and see your success, the easier you will find it to persevere. The more you persevere, the closer you will come to your goals and the easier it will be to stay focused. The process is cyclical.

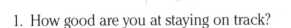

Practice Session

1. How good are you at staying on track?

What might you do to improve your ability to stay focused?

2. What was the last major mistake you made?

What did you learn from it?

3. How might you become more flexible in making a mid-course correction in your life?

4. Is there a negative experience that you are working to overcome? What ideas from this chapter might you apply to your life to help you transform negatives into positives?

5. How good are you at persevering? Respond to the following questions with a yes or no answer:

   A. My first project of the day (in the office, at home, in school) earned my steady attention until it was completed.
   ☐YES ☐NO

   B. My family knows that determination and perseverance are qualities that have characterized my life this day.
   ☐YES ☐NO

   C. Aches and pains failed to deter me in my specific duties for the day.
   ☐YES ☐NO

   D. While sentiment might have led me to relax, discipline in my own life as well as toward my loved ones caused me to persevere in what seemed right to me.
   ☐YES ☐NO

E. Although at times I was disillusioned by others and tempted to withdraw from such wholesome activities as church boards and PTA, I continued to participate.
☐ YES ☐ NO

F. Encouragement in my chosen line of endeavor was clearly lacking today, but I persisted in doing that which I felt to be right.
☐ YES ☐ NO

G. Nothing deterred me from pursuing all of the details relative to my rightful duties for this day.
☐ YES ☐ NO

H. Despite a lack of genuine desire to continue my personal reading and reflection, I stuck with it, knowing that it was the right thing to do.
☐ YES ☐ NO

I. Today I have kept in mind these deep healthy desires, which I know help strengthen the roots of my principles and beliefs.
☐ YES ☐ NO

Now, go back and consider any NO responses you made. Those are areas in which you need to work on balance and goals. Those are the areas that may be most likely to derail you and keep you from achieving the success you desire. Make a renewed effort to come up with all "YES" responses tomorrow! A commitment to persevere needs to be renewed daily.

Giving and Growing

Becoming a Generous and Prosperous Person

She opens her mouth with wisdom.
On her tongue is the law of kindness.

—KING SOLOMON

One day while waiting for a delayed flight at an airport gate, Kristin Rhyne found herself fuming. She had places to be and important things to do. The delay was a waste of her time…and then she thought to herself, *It doesn't need to be a waste!* She began to jot down a business plan for turning this inconvenience into an opportunity.

At the time, Kristin was a student at the Harvard Business School. The idea she came up with while waiting in an airport soon became a real business. She raised $750,000 from friends and family members to start Polished, Inc. She opened her first Polished store at Boston's Logan International Airport, selling top-of-the-line beauty products and services. At Polished, a woman could get a manicure, pedicure, or massage while she waited for her flight. Soon, Kristin's Polished stores could be found in busy airports all across the United States. A long airport wait—made even more likely these days with the amount of time suggested for security checks—can be turned into a time of personal pampering. Rather than be frustrated at a delayed or cancelled flight, a woman can emerge from the experience feeling refreshed and comforted. What a concept![1]

In most cases, a woman need only look at the flip side of an annoying problem, a reoccurring nuisance, or a repeated struggle to find an opportunity for GIVING. It may appear on the surface that Kristin Rhyne just had a good business idea. Not so! She saw a NEED. In that need, she found an opportunity to GIVE a service to women—in her case, women who were traveling and tired. The truth is, embedded in every NEED is an opportunity to GIVE, and embedded in every opportunity to give is a GOOD IDEA for a product, service, or mission of caring!

The Link Between Giving and Growing

I mentioned in the introductory chapter that I linked the musical note "G" to two words, Giving and Growing, because these two words are inevitably intertwined. When you give out of a generous heart, you WILL grow as a person. You WILL grow in your feelings of joy, contentment, and fulfillment. Those who grow as a result of giving have an even greater desire to give. This is one of life's basic cycles.

We don't have to make the growth happen if we will simply make the giving happen. And where do we start? By identifying a NEED and moving immediately to GIVE of ourselves in a way that will meet that need.

That's what Helen did.

Helen's husband left a lucrative government job, packed up Helen and their three small children, and moved to the country, where he was determined to be a cattle rancher. Helen was unsure about the ranching but she did agree that it was a good idea to raise their children in a rural environment. She remembers thinking at the time, *If things get rough, at least we'll always have food. No one ever starved eating steak.*

Things didn't turn out exactly as Helen had thought they would. After five years and four more children, she and her family were struggling more than ever. Besides raising cattle her husband was farming to grow the feed for his herd. Once, while sitting on a tractor, his wallet fell out of his back pocket and he plowed it under. It contained the last sixteen dollars the family had. The wallet wasn't plowed up again for many years. Another time, her husband accidentally mixed turnip seed in with the hayseed. That year the family ate a lot of turnips. They also ate a lot of rabbit and squirrel meat because they needed to sell all the beef they could to make ends meet. They were definitely not eating steak every night!

Finally, Helen and her husband decided they couldn't survive this rural life unless he went back to work. He found another government job, which left Helen to care for seven children and a herd of cows. While she was an expert at detecting the slightest sniffle in her children, she wasn't as adept at diagnosing the health of their cattle. That first winter with Helen in charge, several head of cattle caught pneumonia and died. She had to break the ice in the nearby creek every morning so the cattle could drink. One morning she didn't break the ice properly and several of the cows walked out on the ice, fell through, and drowned. These losses were a major setback.

Helen changed her game plan. She and her husband decided that HE would stay home and take care of the cattle and raise the children while SHE went back to work. No local employers would give her a job, primarily because they all thought she should stay at home, be a full-time wife and mother, and insist her husband work. She finally drove the only car the family had to a larger town thirty miles away and there, she parked the car out of sight—primarily because it was an old hearse—and began to call upon several oil companies.

After she filled out the first application, giving the names and ages of all her children as the form required, the person evaluating her application said, "Honey, I can't submit this application to any of our departments. You have too many young children. We couldn't possibly depend on you to be here regularly."

Helen left the building feeling devastated, but she also was determined to make a creative adjustment in her game plan for getting a job. She wrote on her next application that she had two elementary-school-aged children (which was true)…and within a week she had a job.

It was hard for Helen to leave her children at home, and equally hard to talk about only two of her children at work, but she was a model employee and after one year she was promoted and given a raise. Eventually Helen corrected her records and added all of her children to her health insurance plan at work, but by that time, her work record was so good nobody cared how many children she had. Over the next several decades Helen developed a lucrative career and became a successful businesswoman. Today, she says she is proud of the meaningful contribution she made to her family. She and her husband raised their children in the environment they believed was best. And all through the years, she remained an attentive, loving mother and wife.

Getting from point A to point B was not a straight line for Helen. I doubt if it's a straight line for any person. Sometimes changes are necessary along the way—in fact, mid-course corrections are the norm for most women I know who have built strong businesses and strong families simultaneously.

Flexibility and Creativity

In the previous chapter we dealt with focus, and disciplining our lives to persevere in maintaining focus. Focus, however, does not mean rigidity. A person must allow for creative insights along the path toward potential, and certainly on the road from failure to success. You must be willing to be:

- **Flexible.** Time and distance are no longer the restraints they used to be. International communication that used to take hours or days can occur in minutes or be in "real time." Virtually anything is possible and virtually anyone can do it. Staying flexible in today's environment while maintaining a core of absolute and universal beliefs is a skill that requires creativity, adaptability, and a willingness to learn from mistakes.

  I find that many people over forty have a decreased capacity to adapt, or to be flexible. Certainly I do not advocate that a person become so flexible in her values and beliefs that she no longer stands for anything—and therefore, is likely to fall for everything! But I DO advocate that a person become flexible in her use of methodology and technology.

  I spend a great deal of my time traveling and I have learned to become flexible when it comes to flight delays and modes of transportation, which on occasion has meant taking a cart instead of a car! I have also become adept at using a satellite cell phone and a laptop computer. While I refuse to leave behind tried-and-true methods that I know continue to work, I also am open to new methods of doing business and producing positive results. If you don't become flexible in the use of methodology and technology, you'll get left behind.

You also need to be willing to adapt to other cultures and to various personalities. Life at times is topsy-turvy, messy, and obscure. You need to be willing to wade into a world of ambiguity and listen and learn from people who have different backgrounds, perspectives, and career fields. This is especially true as our world continues to "shrink" and cultures are increasingly intermingled.

- **Risk-Taking.** You need to be willing to take a risk, even if it holds the potential for failure. In many cases, highly successful people have said they learned as much or more from their failures as from their successes—and believe me, every successful person has had failure at some point in his or her past.

  Certainly a risk can and should be a "calculated" risk, but giving to meet a need doesn't require very much calculation. At least two people are always going to be better off when you give generously and with a pure heart to meet a genuine need: the recipient of your gift and YOU.

Infuse Your Communication with a Giving Attitude

Much is said in our world about failures in communication. Without a doubt, a failure in communication can be very costly in terms of both dollars and time. A failure in communication can also be devastating to a relationship. One of the best insights I have ever had into success in communication is this: Enter into any conversation looking for an opportunity to give, to help, to care.

Many people approach communication with the attitude, "I need to tell others what I think with openness, honesty, and trust." That certainly is one aspect of communication, but the greater starting point in communication is this perspective: "I want to understand another person to the point that I feel empathy for their feelings and circumstances, accept them for who they are, and hear what it is that they are saying." The concepts of openness, honesty, and trust are no less important. The difference lies in whether you see yourself primarily as a speaker or a listener.

Seek to be a listener! As one person noted many years ago, "We were given two ears and only one mouth. Perhaps God meant for us to listen twice as much as we speak."

Recognize that much of what you communicate to others is expressed through the tone in which you speak and the body language that accompanies your words. Interestingly, researchers have concluded that communication is

- 7 percent words
- 38 percent tone of voice
- 55 percent body language

Through the years I have done a great deal of public speaking, and I have also listened to thousands of speeches. I can always tell how comfortable someone is with the material they are presenting by their body language. If a woman is grasping the podium with white knuckles, shifting back and forth on her feet, and reading her speech, I know she is uncomfortable and afraid. She may have a wonderful speech, but her audience will have difficulty hearing her message because she is uncomfortable in delivering it.

Become aware of your own tone of voice—the volume with which you speak, the forcefulness of your expression, and the strain that may be accompanying your words. Become aware of how you handle your entire body as you speak.

Always be open to clarification and questions. Ask for clarification of statements that you don't understand. Ask questions to get ALL the information you need. At the same time, don't resent it when others seek clarification or ask questions of you. Be patient in your explanations and your restatements.

I truly believe that clarification of message is at the heart of conflict resolution. In other words, I believe the foremost reason we have so much misunderstanding and hard feelings both at home and in the workplace is that we haven't taken the time or made the effort to clarify what we *mean* by the words we speak.

Let me share with you nine ways in which you can GIVE through communication:

1. **Give a View into Your Soul.** Offer your opinions and ideas with vulnerable transparency. Genuine caring and vulnerability are marks of "high-level" communication. Low-level communication is habitual, rote, or rooted in gossip. It is at a LOW level of communication that we relay "facts" and engage in polite exchanges that actually have very little meaning. We all know the "Hi, how are you?" question that is followed by the "I'm fine. How are you?" answer. Neither person may be fine, but the communication is so shallow that neither party is willing to admit or to hear true feelings!

   High-level communication deals with opinions, feelings, and real transparency and honesty in expressing desires, dreams, strengths, faults, flaws, and weaknesses. High-level communication involves some vulnerability and risk. It is the level at which genuine caring is both felt and given.

   It is vitally important that you be willing to risk the expression of ALL that you are. The more you are willing to take this risk, the more others will open up to you and share with you their strongest opinions, their deepest feelings, and their greatest desires and problems.

2. **Give Your Trust.** True intimacy in caring and communication requires trust. Choose to trust others and to take what they say at face value. You may be hurt from time to time, but your transparency in trust will also express to the world at large, "I am an honest person. The caring that I express is not self-centered

or manipulative. I truly desire the best for you." Have a heart that makes room for others. It is the key to being effective in caring.

3. **Give Way to Others.** There are times when you must yield to others. No matter how strong a leader you are, there are times when you must be a follower. If you are a natural follower, there may be times when you need to rise up and lead. Relationships involve give and take. They also involve one person taking the lead from time to time, and another person following that lead with enthusiasm and without any resentment, bitterness, or jealousy.

4. **Give Uplifting Encouragement.** One of the greatest needs I see in our world today is a need for encouragement. The core of all encouragement is the compliment. Mark Twain once said, "I can live for two months on a good compliment." Heartfelt, genuine compliments have a strong motivating power. A compliment can change the way you see yourself, and also the way you see the world around you.

I had a drama teacher in high school who greatly encouraged me. She gave me parts in school plays and told me I could do *anything* I set my heart and mind to do. I believed her. Her positive words had a lifelong impact.

5. **Give Positive Compliments.** Many women have *never* had a person consistently speak positive words into their lives. Countless people have been brought up in homes where they were told repeatedly that they would not and could not succeed. Over time, they bought that lie, internalized it, and are living out the negative perceptions of the person who spoke the lie.

All that can change! If there's nobody around you to speak positive encouragement to you, speak it to yourself! Don't wait on this. Start today to tell yourself the GOOD things you can do and are. At the same time, begin to give sincere compliments to others. I'm not talking about statements of flattery or words limited to a person's appearance. Speak to the inner qualities of character that you see in a person. The more you give compliments to others, the more you will feel encouragement within yourself.

6. **Give Expressions of Confidence.** Part of encouraging others involves expressing confidence in another person's ability, ideas, or enthusiasm. Say to a person, "Hey, I believe in you," or, "I see great leadership potential in your life," or, "I believe you will help change this world," or, "Your commitment to excellence inspires me."

7. **Give Words of Comfort.** Seek to comfort people who are discouraged or sorrowful. Words of comfort are especially needed in times of divorce, death, or loss, including loss of a business or career. Remember, however, that words are not the only way to give comfort. Sometimes your actions will speak volumes.

8. **Give Patient Instruction.** I mentioned earlier the need to remain flexible in learning new technology. From my own experience, I can tell you that it's possible to learn new technology, but it can also be difficult!

   My daughter Debi was my first "computer teacher." I grew up in an age of typewriters, copy machines that were actually hand-cranked miniature presses (mimeograph machines), and messy carbon paper. During our first lesson, Debi gave me such an overload of information that I was about to give up. Debi assumed that I knew what words like "menu," "icon," and "mouse" meant. Well, I knew those words, of course—they related to food, religious art, and small rodents! Finally I said to Debi, "Listen, I need for you to be patient with me."

   Fortunately for me, Debi *was* patient. She slowly took me through the steps and procedures, and today I can surf the Web almost as well as I surfed the waves of Waikiki in the 1960s.

   The fact is, I consider patience to be a valuable *principle* that is absolutely essential for good relationships and good communication. I want to live with patience for others, even if they are slow to adopt the principles and values that I *know* are right! Make patience a gift from your heart.

9. **Give Expressions of Hope.** Do your utmost to express hope to those who are in need or are facing negative situations.

I recently heard about two women who had very different problems. One of the women had been abandoned by her husband, who had become blatantly involved in an adulterous affair. The other woman had been diagnosed with cancer. These two women attended the same church, and they immediately responded to each other with genuine friendship. They began meeting regularly just to talk and they made a pact to be "Hopeful Friends" to each other.

The woman with cancer had an excellent marriage. The woman with the bad marriage had excellent health. They each gave to the other out of their strengths, and in helping each other, they both found that their own problems began to be resolved. They remain great friends nearly ten years later. The woman with cancer has been in full remission for eight years now. The woman with marriage problems has been through a divorce, has remarried, and has a darling child and a happy life.

These two women both chose to believe the best for each other…and over time, they experienced the best in their own lives as well. They grew as they gave!

Seize the Opportunity to Serve

A number of years ago I was on my way to South Africa when my plane was late for a connecting flight. About thirty of us were unable to reschedule and since our plane had been one of the last to arrive at the airport, we were given vouchers for nearby hotels and restaurants. I must admit I didn't have a very good attitude about the circumstance in which I found myself.

As I was trying to reschedule my trip, I overheard the elderly gentleman in front of me say quietly to the agent, "The reason I need to get out tonight is that my wife is dying of cancer and they don't think she will make it through the night."

I immediately felt ashamed. How important was a business seminar in Africa compared to a man losing his wife and being unable to be with her in her last hours on this earth?

The agent was sorry, but there was nothing she could do for this man. She handed us both vouchers for the same hotel and restaurants. On the way to the hotel, the man turned to me and said, "Would you mind having dinner with me?"

"I'd like to have dinner with you," I replied. By this time, it was nearly midnight. We went to a little coffee shop and he began to pour out his life to me, telling me all about how he and his wife met and fell in love, and then about their children. He had been a United States congressman for many years and had retired and built a home in a lovely resort area. His wife had been visiting their daughter when she suddenly had taken a turn for the worse in her battle against cancer.

I listened and tried to be a friend to this man I had just met. I told him my prayers would be with him through the night. Early the next morning we met in the lobby to return to the airport. He told me in his quiet voice that his wife had died during the night.

I learned a valuable lesson that night about what it means to focus on *people* rather than *schedules*. My flight to Africa was better than expected—on board were two of my good friends and we had a wonderful time visiting on the long journey. In all, the trip had meaning and significance I can't imagine it having otherwise.

Now when flights are delayed or cancelled I take a deep breath and begin to look around to see what opportunities I might find to help someone near me.

I get a lot of e-mails. One of the best stories I have ever received was this one:

Twenty years ago, I drove a cab for a living. It was a cowboy's life, a life for someone who wanted no boss. Because I drove the night shift, my cab became a moving confessional. Passengers climbed in, sat behind me in total anonymity and told me about their lives. I encountered people whose lives amazed me, ennobled me, and made me laugh and weep. But none touched me more than a woman I picked up late one August night.

I was responding to a call from a small brick four-plex in a quiet part of town. I assumed I was being sent to pick up some partiers or someone who had just had a fight with a lover or a worker heading to an early shift at some factory in the industrial part of town.

When I arrived at 2:30 A.M. the building was dark except for a single light in a ground floor window. Under these circumstances many drivers would just honk once or twice, wait a minute, then drive away. But I had seen too many impoverished people who depend on taxis as their only means of transportation. Unless a situation smelled of danger, I always went to the door. *This passenger might be someone who needs my assistance,* I reasoned to myself.

So I walked to the door and knocked.

"Just a minute," answered a frail, elderly voice. I could hear something being dragged across the floor. After a long pause, the door opened. A small woman in her eighties stood before me.

She was wearing a print dress and a pillbox hat with a veil pinned on it. She looked like someone from a 1940s movie. By her side was a small nylon suitcase.

The apartment looked as if no one had lived in it for years. All the furniture was covered with sheets. There were no clocks on the walls, no knick-knacks or utensils on the counters. In the corner was a cardboard box filled with photos and glassware.

"Would you carry my bag out to the car?" she asked.

I took the suitcase to the cab, then returned to assist the woman. She took my arm and we walked slowly toward the curb. She kept thanking me for my kindness.

"It's nothing," I told her. "I just try to treat my passengers the way I would want my mother treated."

When we got in the cab she gave me an address, then asked, "Could you drive through downtown? It's not the shortest way but I'm not in a hurry. I don't have any family left and the doctor says I don't have very long, so I'm on my way to a hospice."

I reached over and turned off the meter. "What route would you like to take?" I asked.

For the next several hours we drove through the city. She showed me the building where she had worked as an elevator operator. We drove through the neighborhood where she and her husband had lived when they were newlyweds. She had me pull up in front of a furniture warehouse that had once been a ballroom where she had gone dancing as a girl. Sometimes she'd ask me to slow in front of a particular building or corner and would just sit staring into the darkness, saying nothing.

As the first hint of sun was creasing the horizon, she suddenly said, "I'm tired. Let's go now."

We drove in silence to the address she had given me. When we arrived two orderlies came out to the cab. They were solicitous and intent, watching her every move, as if they had been expecting her. When I opened the trunk and removed her suitcase she was already seated in a wheelchair.

"How much do I owe you?" she asked, reaching for her purse.

"Nothing," I said.

"You have to make a living," she said.

"There are other passengers," I replied. Almost without thinking I bent and gave her a hug. She held on to me tightly.

"You gave an old woman a moment of joy," she said. "Thank you."

I squeezed her hand, and then walked into the dim morning light. Behind me a door shut. It was the sound of the closing of a life. I didn't pick up any more passengers that day. I finished my shift driving aimlessly, lost in thought. What if that woman had gotten an angry driver, or one who was impatient to end his shift? What if I had refused to take the run or had honked once then driven away? I don't think I've done anything more important in my life. We're conditioned to think that our lives revolve around great moments, but great moments often catch us unaware, beautifully wrapped in what others may consider a small moment.

I love that example. A man who was trying to make a living gave up the chance to make an extra buck because he saw an opportunity to help someone else. The old woman's request to drive around town interfered with the driver's ability to pick up other passengers, but he embraced the interference.

Tapping into Your Ability to Give

One of the things I've learned about women through the years is that most of them have an amazing ability to give of themselves. Many, of course, give of themselves tirelessly to help their children, spouse, parents, co-workers, and friends. Other women also find it within themselves to help people they don't even know—and in some cases, even their enemies.

Elizabeth of Hesse-Darmstadt was born a German Hessian princess. As a child she was raised in England in the court of her grandmother, Queen Victoria. At age twenty she married the brother of Czar Alexander III of Russia, the Grand Duke Sergei Alexandrovich. She became the Grand Duchess Elizabeth. As a member of the royal family she was surrounded by luxury and affluence. Elizabeth, however, had a heart for the poor in her community. When her husband was appointed governor of Moscow she spent her time satisfying her social obligations and visiting hospitals, prisons, and orphanages. She did what she could to narrow the gap between the rich and the poor in early-twentieth-century Russia.

Russia at that time was not the safest place to be. Civil war was imminent. Terrorism against the Czar and his family was common and eventually the Grand Duke was assassinated. Elizabeth continued her work. On the day of her husband's funeral she arranged for free meals to be served to Moscow's poor. She also visited her husband's assassin in prison and even asked her brother-in-law, Czar Nicholas, to pardon him.

After her husband's death Elizabeth's life changed forever and so did she. She gave away almost all of her jewelry and sold her most luxurious possessions so she could open the Martha and Mary home in Moscow, a religious community for women committed to serving the poor. Within a few years Elizabeth and seventeen other women were dedicated as "Sisters of Love and

Mercy." She said, "I am leaving a glittering world where I had glittering position, but with all of you I am descending into a greater world—the world of the poor and the suffering." The Sisters opened a hospital, orphanage, library, and school. During the next decade, their work grew as they helped hundreds of poor and suffering Russian citizens in and around Moscow. The best doctors and nurses worked in their hospital without charging for their services. During World War I the Sisters helped care for wounded soldiers.

Then came the revolution. The Bolsheviks spared the convent at first, but soon Elizabeth was arrested. She spent months in prison before she was thrown in an abandoned mine shaft to die. Just before she died she was heard singing a hymn from the liturgy.[2]

Today Saint Elizabeth is remembered in stone on the west front of Westminster Abbey. It was her name I gave to the rector, asking him to place my bouquet of flowers by her memorial at the time of Princess Diana's funeral. Whenever I visit London I make a point of going to Westminster Abbey for a Vespers service. I love to hear the Boys Choir sing, and then I pause to pay respect at Elizabeth's memorial and to remember what it means to be a woman who gives herself away to others.

Where Will You Give?

Start where you are. Care for the people with whom you come in contact TODAY. Care for those in your own home…in your place of work…in your neighborhood…in your church. Start giving yourself away. Communicate at deeper levels with a trusting heart and sincere compliments. Listen and seek to understand. Do what it is that you can do, and if a project is too big for you to handle alone, enlist the help of others to build a caring team.

There's plenty of need in this world—at times and in places it is mountainous in size! Dive in and care to the best of your ability.

With Whom Will You Give?

The more you focus on caring for other people, the more you will discover real intimacy in relationships. People who care develop an amazing bond with those who receive their care. People who care *as a team* also build a strong and enduring bond of friendship. One of the most positive things I believe you can do as a family is to turn your family into a "team" that cares for a particular group of people in need.

As I have traveled the world in building my business and speaking at conferences, I have come in contact with hundreds of people who, over the course of any given year, are doing amazing projects to rebuild their communities and nations. Those who "care" have become my strongest associates, and I can't help but notice that they are also among my most successful leaders. They are the ones who demonstrate the greatest morale, self-motivation, and enthusiasm for all areas of their lives.

I first learned the principle of teamwork in music. When you are performing in an ensemble you must rely on all the other members of the ensemble to follow the conductor, play their parts, and perform to the best of their ability. The same is true for families, companies, churches, and communities.

Successful teams are built on two key principles:

1. **Unity.** The vision for a caring project must be articulated clearly and fully. Every person should have a good understanding of *who* is being helped and *why*.

   There's a difference between uniformity and unity. There's also a difference between a union and unity. Uniformity says everybody does the same thing in the same way. Union says that two people are in association, such as a marriage or business partnership. Unity, however, says that all people involved in a project or caring mission have the same *goal* and the same basic understanding of the reason they are pursuing that goal. There should still be room for individuality and creativity—not everyone on a team can or should take the same role. Every person, however, should have a role through which he or she can contribute his or her best, be encouraged to give as much as he or she is able, and receive expressions of value and appreciation from all involved.

2. **Commitment.** Each person must be committed to the mutual goal and to other team members. It is very important that team members be encouraged to build up one another in times of setback, delay, or struggle.

I first learned about Huldah Buntain and her husband, Mark, in the late 1980s. By the time I met Huldah she and Mark had served for many years as missionaries in Calcutta, India. They had a strong, healthy association with the Indian people. Their ministry included a school and a hospital.

While Huldah was in the United States visiting family and friends in 1989, she received word that Mark had experienced a brain hemorrhage and was undergoing surgery. She did her best to return to Calcutta immediately but no flight was available until the next afternoon. Early the next morning she received a call informing her that Mark had died.

Huldah flew back to Calcutta that afternoon with a heavy heart. At the airport hundreds of parishioners were waiting for her. More than twenty thousand people turned out for Mark's funeral. They crowded the streets and rooftops to pay their respects. The outpouring of support overwhelmed and comforted Huldah, but she was also frightened about the future. Could she lead these people alone? How could she stay in Calcutta? Others around her were also eager to know what would happen in the future.

Several days after Mark's funeral, Mother Teresa came to Huldah to offer her condolences, and to invite her to a memorial service to be held at *her* mission in Mark's honor. About that same time other church leaders in North India met and elected Huldah to take Mark's place as senior pastor of the church the Buntains had established in Calcutta. Huldah had been ordained almost twenty years before; now the time had come to dust off the certificate and begin to use it again. The first sermon she delivered after Mark's death was titled "Carry On!"

Over the next few months Huldah was nearly overwhelmed by the many responsibilities she faced, even as she continued to grieve the loss of her beloved husband. She knew she could not do everything herself—she needed the team of doctors and nurses, schoolteachers and administrators, church laymen and staff members, pastors and missionaries, to carry on the work. She finally saw herself not as the person responsible for the work, but as the leader of a TEAM of people. Believe me, it takes a team to feed the more than twenty thousand women and children their ministry feeds each day, as well as to care for thousands in the hospital and to teach more than ten thousand children.[3]

I support Huldah's work. Her life challenges me, and her mission has become part of *my* mission. I have toured her hospital and visited with her there—I am committed to helping her build a new wing on the hospital. Certainly I can't do that alone…I, too, am building a TEAM of people to help me.

And that's the way caring goes. One person leads a team that requires team members to establish teams, and so forth until the totality of a need is met. The greater the drive to care, the larger the mission tends to grow, and the larger the mission, the more people that are required to carry it on and make it successful.

In becoming a caring person, don't feel as if you need to do all the work yourself. Build a team that is unified and committed.

The Great Rewards of Serving

One of life's universal laws is that you get out of life what you put into it. If you give your time and energy to the people who help run your business, you get back productivity and prosperity. When you reach out to people outside your business, such as neighbors, friends, and others in your community who are in need, you create for yourself a balanced life in which work is just one aspect of *service*.

The genuinely successful life is a life in which you seek to make a difference in all the lives you touch on a regular, daily basis. That includes how you respond to the person who fills your car with gasoline, rings up your purchases at the grocery store, mows your lawn, cleans your house, sits next to you in church, helps you in your workout at the gym, and so forth.

Wherever you go and whatever you do, look for ways to serve others. Ask yourself continually, "What can I do to help?" The more you turn yourself inside-out for others, the more you will generate your own peace, joy, fulfillment, satisfaction, and authentic success.

Instead of planning your day around work goals, plan your day around service.

Practice Session

1. Identify two people whom you regard as your role models in caring. What specifically have they done? Which of their traits do you hope to incorporate into your own life?

   A.

   B.

2. Identify one person you know who fits the description for each of the phrases below.

    · A person who is discouraged:

    · A person who may be questioning her ability or her efforts:

    · A person who needs comforting:

For each person you name above, identify a specific positive, encouraging thing you might do to help that person in the coming week.

3. Name six people whom you know NEED you at home or at work. Next to each name, write one special thing you might do to express your love and care this week:

A. _____

_____

_____

B. _____

_____

_____

C. _____

_____

_____

D. _____

_____

_____

E. _____

_____

_____

F. _____

_____

_____

4. Read aloud this poem by Mother Teresa to your children, or to a group of children you know. Talk to them about what it means to be a caring person.

> When I was homeless, you opened your doors,
> When I was naked, you gave me your coat.
>
> When I was weary, you helped me find rest,
> When I was anxious, you calmed all my fears.
>
> When I was little, you taught me to read,
> When I was lonely, you gave me your love.
>
> When in a prison, you came to my cell,
> When on sick bed, you cared for my needs.
>
> In a strange country, you made me at home.
> Hurt in a battle, you bound up my wounds.
> Searching for kindness, you held out your hand.
>
> When I was Negro, or Chinese, or White,
> Mocked and insulted you carried my cross.
>
> When I was aged, you bothered to smile,
> When I was restless, you listened and cared.
>
> You saw me covered with spittle and blood,
> You knew my features, though grimy with sweat.
>
> When I was laughed at, you stood by my side,
> When I was happy, you shared in my joy. [4]

— MOTHER TERESA

Playing
All the
Notes

CHAPTER

9

Let me quickly recap the "notes" we've covered in this book:

A = Action. Seize the moment and sustain your forward motion. You will never reach your potential if you sit in the audience of life and never become part of the choir on stage!

B = Balance. Life is a composite of at least eight basic components. To live a genuinely successful life, you need to pursue your potential in EACH of these eight areas: family, work, spiritual life, emotional health, friends, learning, finances, and physical health. Find what satisfies EVERY facet of life fully and peacefully.

C = Character. Choose to pursue life's BEST and build your life on values and beliefs that reflect the highest and noblest absolutes.

D = Destiny. Develop a personal mission statement for your life. Define your potential and set goals related to that definition.

E = Energy. Explore and develop the central core of your own spirituality. That will be the power source for the pursuit of your potential.

F = Focus. Make creative adjustments to stay on track. Discipline yourself to persevere through tough times, always staying focused on the "big picture" of your own destiny.

G = Giving and Growing. As you become an increasingly generous person, you will grow and become prosperous in *all* areas of your life. As you get closer and closer to your full potential, you'll discover that you have more and more to give.

These notes need to be played FULLY. By working them together into a whole, you will make a melody that will bring joy to your smile, peace to your heart, and fulfillment to your life. Embrace your

family and friends and work associates as you develop these concepts in your life. Learn to sing a beautiful harmony with others.

I have no doubt you can do it. In fact, I *expect* you to do it.

Chapter 2

1 Renee Bondi and Nancy Curtis, *The Last Dance but Not the Last Song* (Old Tappan, NJ: Fleming H. Revell Company, 2002).

2 A'Lelia Bundles, *On Her Own Ground: The Life and Times of Madam C. J. Walker* (New York: Scribner, 2001), 25, 189–190, 231.

3 Information about Elisa Pritzker (Highland Community Arts Center), Highland, NY, can be found at her Web site: www.pritzkerstudio.com.

4 Miles Corwin, "With Honors," *Rosie*, October 2001, 58–61.

Chapter 3

1 Quoted in Harold Kushner, *When Everything You've Ever Wanted Isn't Enough* (NY: Simon & Schuster, 1986), 145.

2 Barbara Benham, "Love of Labor," *Working Woman*, May 2001, 19.

3 Lauren Slater, "The Patient Who Healed Me," *Rosie*, November 2001, 57–68.

Chapter 5

1 Janita Poe, "Investing in Futures," *The Atlanta Journal-Constitution,* April 29, 2001, 1.

2 J.Y. Smith and Noel Epstein, "Katherine Graham, a Pillar in U.S. Journalism," *International Herald Tribune*, July 19, 2001, 3.

3 Janet Van Eeden-Harrison, "A Woman of Vision," *Fairlady*, August 1, 2001, 42–44.

4 Amy Wilentz, "Jewel in the Crown," *O, The Oprah Magazine*, August 2001, 150.

5 Ibid.

6 Ibid., 151.

7 Ibid.

8   Gabrielle Studenmund, "50 Ways to Give Back," *More*, December 2001/January 2002, 102.

9   Ibid., 98.

10   Ibid., 99.

Chapter 6

1   Angelique du Toit, "Effective Parenting Necessitates Balance," *Smile Family Club Chronicle*, March 2001, 1.

2   Anne Morrow Lindbergh, *A Gift from the Sea* (NY: Pantheon Books, 1991), 16.

Chapter 7

1   See www.celcee.edu/abstracts/c20002295.html.

2   To learn more about Stephanie Fast and her incredible story, contact Destiny Ministries, P.O. Box 6081, Aloha, OR 97007 or dfastdm@cs.com.

3   See www.csupomona.edu.

4   David McCullough, *John Adams* (NY: Simon & Schuster, 2001), 169.

Chapter 8

1   FSB, May 2001, p. 60.

2   *Christian Martyrs of the Twentieth Century*, published by Westminster Abbey, designed and printed by Beric Tempest, Great Britain, 1999.

3   You can learn more about Huldah Buntain and the Calcutta Mission of Mercy in her biography, *Woman of Courage*, by Hal Donaldson and Kenneth M. Dobson (Sacramento, CA: Onward Books, 1995).

4   Malcolm Muggeridge, *Something Beautiful for God* (NY: Ballantine Books, 1971), 58.

About the Author

Beverly Sallee is an internationally recognized businesswoman, inspirational speaker, musician, and philanthropist.

Beverly holds a Bachelor of Arts degree in piano and a Master of Arts degree in choral conducting. In 1978, she found herself at a crossroads in her life. She had been teaching at the university level for ten years, and was struggling to juggle her commitments as a wife, mother, student, piano teacher, choral conductor, music professor, and volunteer but she felt herself at a dead-end financially. With a strong desire to give her children a better life and an excellent education, she began a part-time direct-marketing business. Her entrepreneurial business grew dramatically and successfully, and by 1985, she had achieved a level that allowed her to leave her university position and pursue her business full-time.

Today, Beverly's business has expanded to forty-nine nations. She continues her passion for music by giving music scholarships all over the world through the Oregon Bach Festival and Stuttgart Bachakademie Germany. She continues to work with Easter Seals on the national level. She is helping build a hospital in Calcutta, India, and is active in the Network of Caring established in association with World Vision.

Beverly's motto is "The world is my home and the sky is the limit." She invites you to soar with her into the first-class echelon, both professionally and personally.